Raymond and Trudy

By Michael Twist

ISBN: 978-0-9885344-7-6

Cover: Dawn Husted
http://dawnhusted.weebly.com
istockphoto.com Robert Mayne File 6611051

To anyone who has ever had it rough growing up, as well as all those who've lent these young people support, understanding, and guidance along the way. Also, to my loving daughters, Lauren and Julie – may your travails be few and your joys many.

M.T.

Short story collections by Michael Twist include:

Twist's Tales

Full of Choices

Touch of Beyond

Elements of Darkness

Short But Seldom Sweet Micro-fiction

info@michael-twist.com

1

Trudy Thomas stomped the dirty snow from the heavy, black combat boots she wore nearly every day. She had been wearing them for nearly her entire junior year after finding the pair, as well as a moldy smelling military issue jacket, in an Army surplus store outside of Reno. The boots had seemed heavy at first, and Trudy wondered about the young man who had worn them. She wondered how many miles he had hiked and if the boots had given him blisters like they had given her. It seemed certain that the young soldier had been small in stature, since the size of his feet nearly matched her own. If the boots had given him blisters, causing his socks to bleed through, Trudy did not feel sorry for him. At least he had come home, unlike her brother Jimmy. Trudy did not want to think where her brother's boots might be. They had not come home either. Every night Trudy had washed the raw, open sores on her heels and little toes. She walked gingerly around her high school campus each day, refusing to go back to the comfortable tennis shoes she had worn before and even after her mother had opened the door to two grave-faced men in uniform.

What was a little discomfort when walking, Trudy reasoned, compared to having your guts purified by a grenade?

Sitting by Trudy's side was her best friend, Rochelle Martz. Rochelle cracked open a can of beer that she had pulled from her shoulder bag. Both girls sat on a picnic table facing the old church across the street from the park they alone occupied. Rochelle plucked the nearly spent cigarette from her mouth and took a long sip from the can before grimacing and replacing the cigarette.

Trudy looked at her friend with a puzzled expression. "If it tastes like hell, why do you drink it?"

"Who said it tastes like hell?" Rochelle replied, the words escaping with the torrent of smoke she exhaled.

"Your expression said it all," Trudy replied, grounding her own cigarette butt into the snow on the seat of the picnic table that featured several terse but decidedly antisocial messages carved into its surface.

"I like the taste, how the carbonation sort of sizzles on your tongue. Like it's angry with whatever passed before it," Rochelle said. "I brought one for you, if you want."

"No thanks," Trudy said. She looked toward the Sierras, which were still snow-capped and visible from where they sat on the outskirts of Carson City. She thought about Rochelle's description and the way her friend had with words. Trudy liked to write poems that never seemed to finish - more like fragments of poems, bits and pieces of words that sounded uncommon and often regal when placed in just the right order. She spent hours at night, just doodling in a spiral notebook, sprawled on her bed with the door locked, waiting for a fight to break out between her mother and Dirk. Despite the time she put into them, the poems never felt right, always as if she were a phrase or even just a single word away from getting it right. And then, more often than not, Rochelle would casually utter a sentence that had more meaning than the entirety of the poem Trudy had spent an evening erasing, revising, and rewording.

Once, Rochelle had described Dirk as having all the personality of a jackhammer, and the thought had stayed with Trudy for days, causing her to have to bite the inside of her cheeks every time she encountered Dirk, for fear that she would laugh in the man's face. It was also Rochelle who had dubbed Mrs. Thomas's boyfriend as Dirkbag, a moniker that had both girls rolling on Rochelle's bedroom floor in peels of laughter for ten minutes, until tears rolled from their heavily mascaraed eyes.

"I can't wait to get out of this hellhole," Rochelle said bitterly. She lit another cigarette with the green plastic Bic lighter she fished out of her trench coat pocket.

Trudy nodded and turned her head as Rochelle nudged her arm, offering another smoke from the nearly depleted pack. A quartet of underclassmen streaked by on their BMX bikes. They looked like oversized circus apes and reminded Trudy of the winged monkeys that once took Dorothy and Toto hostage. "Yeah," Trudy agreed. "As far away as possible," she concluded.

"Where we can open up a salon and play our music as loud as we want while cutting and styling hair all day," Rochelle added, before taking a long sip of her beer.

Trudy smiled at her friend. She looked at the dirty brown roots that had supplanted the sable hair on Rochelle's scalp and knew that her own head looked no different, since they had taken turns dying one another's hair on an afternoon when the idea had

sounded infinitely more fun than attending social studies with Mr.
Burns.

Getting away from Carson City, and even Nevada, sounded
good to Trudy. Hanging out with her best friend was also pleasant.
But Trudy wasn't sure she wanted to spend her life washing,
cutting, setting, and drying other people's hair. All the same, it was
not a sentiment she cared to share with Rochelle, who had her
heart set on the notion since moving into the same trailer park at
the end of the previous summer and befriending Trudy in the full-
throttle way that the friendless are known to adopt and then cling
to one another. "I just want a fresh start," Trudy said, smoke
intermingling with breath that was also visible, due to the
temperature.

"Away from your mom?"

"Yeah, her and the Dirkbag," Trudy replied, a smile
playing on her black lipstick. "Fine father figure that he is."

"At least he's on the outside," Rochelle mused.

Trudy knew that Rochelle was referring to her own father,
who was not likely to be freed from Folsom State Prison before she
was thirty. "At least you knew yours," Trudy responded with a
mocking tone of one-upmanship.

"You got me there, Truds," Rochelle conceded.

It was quiet as both girls thought of their fathers. Jimmy
hadn't had anything nice to say about Trudy's father, Gary, but
refused to trash him around his little sister, mostly, Trudy
supposed, because his own had been no better. Trudy had tried to

talk to her mother any number of times in an effort to learn more about the man who had abandoned his family shortly after Trudy's second birthday, an event for which he had arrived empty-handed. He had failed to bring Trudy a present in much the same way as he had failed to give her his last name.

When Angela Thomas was sober she spoke of the man as the devil, berating his memory with cruel and cutting depictions. Strangely though, when the woman was drunk her memory of Gary Brody usually softened and often took on a bittersweet air of nostalgia, always culminating in tears. It was on these nights that Trudy resorted to covering the woman, curled like a fetus, with a blanket, leaving Angela on the couch, or sometimes even the floor, to awaken in a foul mood as her throbbing head demanded coffee, silence, and aspirin in roughly that order.

Sensing her friend's dispirited sadness, Rochelle put her arm around Trudy and offered, "Your uncle doesn't seem like a bad guy."

"He's okay," Trudy admitted.

"Hey, he gave us jobs at his deli, didn't he?" Rochelle insisted.

"Yeah, I guess so." Trudy began to brighten.

"And we get to work together all summer. Just you and me serving soup, sandwiches, and our own brand of super sultry sexiness," Rochelle chimed in singsong fashion.

Giggles overtook Trudy as she tried to respond. "Just how in the world is serving soup and sandwiches even remotely sexy?"

"I don't know, but we'll find a way. You just watch, sister. It'll be the best summer ever," Rochelle insisted. Both girls laughed at the thought of showing a bit of cleavage as they served bowls of vegetable beef soup to wide-eyed geriatrics.

*If it can be said, in some parts of the country, that football is a
religion, then Coburn, Pennsylvania is such a place.*

Elmore Robinson

2

Cougar coach Jack Parson had a good feeling about next
year's squad as he watched his high school PE class run around the
track on the first sunny spring day of 1977. Several of his players
were tossing the ball around on the field as they had made short
work of the required running. Soon they would embark on a game
of flag football, while the girls continued walking the track,
feigning disinterest in the game and its participants.

Clipboard in hand, Parson was heading to the bleachers to
sit in the sun and watch when the new kid came out of the locker
room and onto the field. He was dressed in cut-off blue jeans and
a well-worn gray sweatshirt, despite having been issued phys. ed.
gear the day before. It was his second day of class, and Parson
had a hunch the kid's locker combination had proven too much for
him again. Instead, the teen handed Parson a late slip from the
counselor.

"O.K. Fine. You're just in time to get in the game,"
Parson said matter-of-factly. The kid studied his teacher's mouth
and looked a little confused. "Go play football," Parson said
slowly.

"I don't know how," the kid managed to say. He had the
sound of someone who could not hear what he was saying and had

been unable to fine-tune his speech in the way that the hearing take for granted.

Parson looked at the young man and smiled empathetically. "Take a few laps, and then just watch for a while until you feel comfortable enough to join the game," the coach said, gesturing in a circuitous fashion. The kid nodded, visibly relieved, and took off in a loping stride.

"Poor kid," Parson mumbled under his breath and sat down on the bleachers to keep an eye on some kids he was looking to start in the fall. The offense was set with Tommy Wilkins returning as starting quarterback. Three good backs mixing speed and power would share time and keep defenses guessing. The offensive line was returning four starters who seemed to spend all their spare time eating and lifting weights. The receiving corps was solid.... Parson noticed the kid running by himself on the track. The girls had all sat down and were plucking at the grass, talking, and watching the game of flag out of the corners of their eyes.

The kid had a long, effortless stride that was both fluid and natural. His mop of flaming red hair seemed to almost float, sponsored by a textbook-smooth gait, the mark of an athlete of some sort. Parson looked at his watch as the kid passed by. Girls had giggled the day before as Parson called, "Raymond Gaines" from his roll sheet. The beleaguered kid looked like he administered his own haircuts with a straight but decidedly upward left to right incline on his crimson bangs. He had appeared awkward, and the lone word out of his mouth indicating his presence sounded far away, consistent with today's speech. But passing by again in little more than a minute's time indicated there was more to this kid than met the eye.

Fifteen minutes later, Parson blew the whistle, and the students lazily trudged back into the gym. Raymond Gaines continued running until Parson began waving and blew the whistle again, louder this time. Scooping his arm through the air in an effort to beckon his new student, Parson smiled. Tommy Wilkins brought the football over to his coach.

"Tommy. Stick around for a second," Parson instructed, flipping the ball back to his quarterback.

"Sure. What's up?" Tommy asked good-naturedly.

"See this kid? I want you to throw the ball around with him for a minute."

"The new kid? He's deaf, you know," Tommy added respectfully.

Parson nodded. "Yeah. I know. I don't need his ears. I just want to see if he's got any hands."

Tommy smiled and turned to the approaching kid, while cocking his arm. He waited until he was sure Raymond saw him before letting loose with an easy toss. The departure from the graceful loping was instantaneous. Raymond awkwardly raised his hands to shield the ball from hitting his face or body, while letting out a squawk like a wounded animal when the pigskin made impact. The ball fell at his feet, and Raymond slowly straightened, looking at Tommy with more hurt than anger.

Tommy put his hands up as if to indicate sincerity. "I'm sorry. I thought you saw me," he said slowly. Raymond nodded, understanding no offense had been intended as he picked up the ball and tossed it back underhanded. Tommy tossed the ball again, and Raymond's attempt to catch the tight spiral yielded results not markedly different from his initial reaction to a ball in flight. Parson had seen enough and pointed to his watch signaling an end to the session. He gave Raymond a good-natured clap on the shoulder as the gangly youth passed on his way into the gym. It was then that the coach realized that Raymond's breathing was no more labored than his own.

As Tommy and his coach walked into the gym the quarterback grinned at his coach. "I guess Markam's still our tight end?"

Parson laughed, "Yeah. His job's safe for now."

Inside the coaches' office, Parson sat down at his desk. Through his window Parson could hear the good-humored grab ass, boasting, and back and forth ribbing as the young men dressed for class after showering. Raymond was sitting on a bench going through his backpack in an effort to avoid social interaction or notice of any kind. He had not showered, his long-sleeved, gray sweatshirt soaked through under the arms and back.

The bell rang, and the students began to file out of the locker room, still talking boisterously. Tommy Wilkins looked

14

back at his coach and waved. Parson beckoned. Tommy came into the coaches' office. He felt honored any time his coach singled him out for discussion. Among Parson's gifts was an ability to raise students, and athletes in particular, to another level, as though *his* expecting great things of them meant *they* should expect the same.

"The new kid. I get the feeling he's got it rough. It'd go a long way with the other kids if you looked after him a little," the coach began.

Tommy looked curious. "He's afraid of the ball. You really think he can play?"

"Don't know. But we're going to try to get him to come out. I'll work on him from my end. You plant the seed from yours. Together, we'll see what we can do," Parson instructed.

"Sure thing coach, but I don't see how he can help us," Tommy said, puzzled as he turned to walk away.

"Hey Tommy," the coach continued. The young quarterback stopped and turned. "He may not be able to help us. But I'm certain *we* can help him."

The quarterback smiled and nodded. He would mull the conversation next period during math and add it to the list of reasons he would walk through fire for his coach.

With Tommy's departure came silence. Parson replayed the scene in his mind, with Raymond shielding his face as if Tommy had sought to hurt or at the very least embarrass the teen. It occurred to Parson that he had witnessed an interaction between both ends of high school's social hierarchy or continuum; with the handsome, gifted, and affable quarterback tossing the leather-stitched symbol that served to define most of the town's adolescent males, to an awkward, likely friendless, newcomer. Even though he knew Gaines was probably more suited to the cross-country team, Parson knew the boy stood a better chance socially if he were to at least to suit up as part of the football team, even if it meant his jersey stood to remain clean. Like it or not, football was what this town - both inside and outside the confines of the high school - revolved around, as surely as fall followed summer each year.

3

Four weeks after Trudy and Rochelle had vowed to have the best summer ever, Trudy walked into her uncle's diner in spirits that matched the warm spring day featuring a host of birds chirping and flowers blooming all around. The end of school was little more than a month away, and Trudy began to anticipate the money she would earn once school got out and she and Rochelle were able to work throughout the week instead of just weekends. Not to mention the camaraderie she and Rochelle would share as they ran the diner during the weekdays, most of their warm summer late evenings free to do with as they pleased. Trudy planned to forgo the wardrobe she knew Rochelle planned on acquiring, in favor of a used car that would grant Trudy a measure of freedom and independence she had never before known. It didn't matter how ugly or beat-up the car was either; just so long as the vehicle was capable of running, Trudy knew that she was as well.

"Hey, girlfriend. Quit padding your bra and get out here," Trudy rang out as she tossed her backpack on the diner's long yellow Formica counter. Trudy's heart nearly stopped when instead of being greeted by the girl with whom she shared dreams, she came upon a slouching, grandfatherly figure in an apron. The man was coming out of the kitchen wiping his hands on a dishtowel.

Both his limp and smile were subtle. "Who needs padding?" the man asked, putting a hand to his chest.

Stopped dead in her tracks, Trudy responded, "Who the hell are you?"

This cold reception did nothing to quell the man's mirthful smile as he returned simply, "I am the hell Carlton."

Trudy could feel the man's eyes taking in her pitch-black hair dye and numerous eyebrow, ear, and lip piercings. "Where's Rochelle?" Trudy asked, a cold feeling overcoming her.

"By Rochelle, I assume you mean the young lady I am replacing. I'm told..."

The cold feeling turned into the sensation of being dunked in a vat of ice. "Replacing? What are you talking about?" Trudy's voice rose noticeably.

"I've been told..." the man resumed his efforts to explain.

Trudy cut him off as tears began to well in her eyes. "Replacing? We're supposed to work together this summer. Me and Rochelle." She felt her chest tighten, panic welling alongside the tears. "We had it all planned out."

The man nodded solemnly, seeing the effect his news had on the teenage girl before him. "Please. If you'd allow me to..."

"Uncle Fritz!" Trudy exclaimed, as the small bell above the front door announced her uncle's entrance.

The middle-aged man, balding and wearing a harrowed expression, took one look at his kid sister's daughter and stated, "You're late, Trudy." Carrying a large, brown paper grocery bag, he walked past his niece and behind the counter to where the man named Carlton stood.

"What happened to Rochelle?" Trudy asked in despair. Her legs suddenly felt heavy, as if gravity had doubled its hold on her.

"She moved," Uncle Fritz said, avoiding eye contact with his niece. "Said her mother got a job in Reno."

Crestfallen, Trudy's voice was nearly a whisper. "She never said anything to me." Rochelle had missed the two previous days of school, telling Trudy over the phone that she had a bad head cold.

"I get the feeling it was a last minute kind of thing," Fritz said. It was clear that he hadn't looked forward to telling Trudy the news.

"I can't believe she didn't tell me," Trudy said, her arms hanging limp at her sides and her chest increasingly feeling as if an elephant was sitting on it.

"I'm sorry, Trudy," her uncle said.

"My summer is so ruined," Trudy said blankly.

"I'm sorry," Fritz repeated, shrugging his shoulders. "I truly am."

Trudy broke from the momentary trance she'd been in and recovered a bit. "Hire someone to replace her," she insisted. Trudy had no other friends to speak of, but she wasn't going to abandon all hope of a summer with someone to talk to.

"I have," Uncle Fritz said.

Trudy looked puzzled.

Only then did Uncle Fritz seem to realize he was standing next to a man Trudy did not know. "Where are my manners? I'm sorry." He looked at them both. "Trudy, this is Carlton Smith. I guess I assumed you'd already met."

"We were just getting acquainted," Carlton said quietly.

"No!" Trudy blurted in denial. "I mean someone real! Someone my age!"

Embarrassed, Uncle Fritz came from behind the counter, took Trudy by the elbow, and led her out the front door. "Trudy, I am truly sorry about Rochelle. I really am. But I just hired Carlton this morning. He's taking the room above the deli. He's seems very dependable."

Fritz's voice was hushed, but Trudy's response could be heard through the glass window. "Dependable? He probably wears Depends!" she shrilled, referring to the television commercials that featured diapers for incontinent adults.

At hearing this, Carlton smiled faintly.

"Look, Trudy, the two of you will be a good combination. He'll bring in the older crowd, and you'll bring in the younger. You two will be able to work any of the shifts, including the morning - after your class. You will make a lot more money. I promise you, it will work out perfectly," Fritz said in a strained voice.

"For you maybe." Trudy pointed through the window at Carlton. "He's a dinosaur! I can't work with him. Couldn't you even hire a girl? Or at least a cute guy *my* age?" she pleaded.

Fritz was losing patience. "Hey, if you don't want the job I can tell your mother it didn't work out," he said, his voice harshening.

"I need the job!" Trudy shrieked, thinking of the car she hoped to purchase.

"Good. Then it's settled. Now, I've got to go." Uncle Fritz gave Trudy a peck on the cheek and left her standing on the sidewalk, tears streaming down her face. Her uncle got in his car and waved goodbye before pulling away from the curb and entering the modest stream of traffic passing by the deli that bore his name.

Trudy stood in front of the door for a full five minutes, her resolve changing from sadness and hurt to a steely resignation. Rochelle had left her without so much as a goodbye, much less an explanation. Why should this be any different, Trudy reasoned. It wasn't as if this hadn't happened to her before. She pushed back the thought of her father pushing her on a swing in the park. The memory had to be wishful thinking after all; no one could remember something from when they were just two. More than likely it was just an image she carried so as to keep from hating her father.

As disappointed as she was, Trudy determined, standing in front of her uncle's deli, not to hate Rochelle for doing this to her. Maybe an explanation was forthcoming. Maybe it was a mistake. Maybe things wouldn't work out, and Rochelle would move back in a week or two. Maybe that was just wishful thinking. After all,

Rochelle, Trudy knew full well, had moved more times than she could count. Maybe to Rochelle, Carson City had just been another stop along the way. Maybe Rochelle had shared the dream of owning a hair salon with a half-dozen other girls over the years.

Before entering the deli, Trudy wiped the tears from her face. She would not give this man, who had replaced her summer companion and confidante, the satisfaction of seeing her wounded. Trudy assumed a spot behind the counter where she found her apron folded neatly in a drawer.

Carlton was washing coffee mugs and placing them on an elevated grill to dry. An awkward silence filled the air until Carlton asked quietly, "You don't think I'm even a little cute?"

For a moment Trudy was tempted to laugh, but the hurt she still felt prevented the reaction that would have eased things for them both. Instead, she snarled, "Go to hell," and walked back toward the kitchen, leaving Carlton to finish lining the thick, white mugs in silence.

"Tempestuous Trudy Thomas," Carlton muttered, as Trudy emerged from the kitchen several moments later. He finished and dried his hands with a dishtowel before extending a handkerchief to Trudy, who still had mascara on her cheek.

"Is that supposed to be funny?" Trudy asked indignantly, ignoring the handkerchief.

Carlton put the square cloth back in his pocket, shrugged his shoulders, and began to unscrew the caps on a tray of salt and pepper shakers. "Merely mildly amusing," he said while suppressing a grin.

"Are you an idiot?" Trudy asked, her hands on her hips and her hackles rising. "You just learn alliteration or something?"

Carlton raised an eyebrow. "Alliteration. I'm impressed," he commented.

"Don't be. It'll probably be the only thing I learn in school this year," Trudy said with a sneer. She pulled a pack of cigarettes out from the back of a drawer behind the counter and lit one with a pink lighter from the same place. When she exhaled with defiance it was in Carlton's direction. He looked at her, his eyebrow still raised, and pointed to a NO SMOKING sign propped on one of the nearby tables. Trudy reached into the sink and retrieved a wet rag before throwing it in the direction of the table. The rag knocked over and partially covered the sign. Trudy raised her right eyebrow to match Carlton's.

"Oops," she said, and held her pack of cigarettes in Carlton's direction. "Want one?" Trudy hoped he would reach for the pack so she could quickly withdraw it.

Carlton's right eyebrow dropped as his left one rose. "No thanks. I never..."

"Yeah, yeah, yeah," Trudy said dismissively, tossing the pack and pink lighter back into the drawer and shoving it closed with her hip.

"So when does it start to get busy around here?" Carlton asked in an effort to change the subject.

"It doesn't," Trudy snorted.

"I see," Carlton returned. He began pouring salt into the salt shakers from a large container with a spout.

It was quiet until Trudy said, "Sometimes I think my uncle just keeps this place open so my mom will stay off his back about me having a job. He doesn't trust me to work in the morning when it's busy."

"Oh, I doubt that's his only reason." Carlton switched to the pepper shakers. "But I'm sure he's glad to be able to help," the old man added.

"It doesn't matter," Trudy said. For a brief moment she was tempted to say something about the car she was hoping to earn, but stopped herself short. This man didn't deserve to know her dreams much less her plans.

"Your uncle tells me you'll be attending summer school," Carlton said. His tone was still cheerful as if repudiating Trudy's.

"What's it to you?" Trudy snapped, a little louder than she meant.

"Very little. I'm sure," Carlton replied, finally subdued.

The old man looked like a dog that had just had its nose slapped, and Trudy felt a tinge of regret, but rather than soften she mimicked him. "Very little. I'm sure." It was quiet while Trudy took the tray of salt and pepper shakers and distributed a pair to each table, aware that Carlton was watching her the entire time. When she returned the empty tray to the counter she said, "It's just one stupid class," her eyes failing to meet Carlton's.

"What are you studying?" he asked gently.

"Lit. If you must know," Trudy said, reaching for a stainless steel napkin box to fill.

Carlton smiled wistfully. "Ah. The world that awaits you," he said with sincerity.

"Will be as boring as you, I'm sure." Trudy dipped her cigarette in the dirty dishwater in the sink before tossing the soggy butt in a garbage can under the counter. "Brace yourself," she said. "Here comes the evening rush."

Carlton turned toward the door where he saw an elderly couple entering. The man held the door open for his wife. He was wearing a gray cardigan and took off his hat upon crossing the threshold. The silver-haired woman waited while he took her coat, folded it over a chair, and pulled hers out for her. It occurred to Carlton that it was the world's loss for having passed this couple by, such simple chivalry no longer commonplace.

Trudy watched the couple, waiting until they were seated before bringing them menus. Carlton wondered for a moment if Trudy had ever seen her father conduct himself toward Trudy's mother the way this man did his wife. "I suppose you need to take a look at the menu, Mr. Renton?" Trudy said, as if offering a well-rehearsed line in a play.

"Please," Mr. Renton responded.

Trudy came back behind the counter and stood next to Carlton. "Gotta look at the menu, but they order the same thing every time. Start cooking a strawberry waffle and a toasted tuna sandwich. I'll pour the milks," she said in a hushed tone.

Carlton looked at his co-worker dubiously. "Just do it," she urged. He turned his back and began to mix the waffle batter after turning on the stove.

"We're ready now, Miss," Carlton heard Mr. Renton say.

Over his shoulder, Carlton watched Trudy pretend to write on a note pad as Mr. Renton ordered a tuna fish sandwich. She continued the scribbling motion as Mrs. Renton said with uncertainty, "I think I'll have the strawberry waffle today."

"And two milks, please," Mr. Renton added.

Trudy nodded solemnly. "You don't say," she murmured, as she added the milks to their order, her pen never touching paper.

Carlton smiled as he poured the batter onto a skillet.

"Have you been crying, dear?" Mrs. Renton asked Trudy, the concern in her voice evident.

Trudy realized her makeup was still in disrepair. "No. Of course not." She jabbed a thumb over her shoulder in Carlton's direction. "The kid and I were just having a water fight when you came in."

Upon hearing this, Carlton turned and waved at the Rentons, a meager smile playing on his lips. Mrs. Renton frowned slightly and handed Trudy her menu.

4

As he had a hundred times a day for the past two years, Coach Parson glanced up at a framed picture on the wall. Three jubilant, senior Cougar linebackers, arms raised in victory as they left the field following the conference title game. Each confident their senior year was but a prelude to what awaited him in life.

Of the three best friends, only Jack Parson had come back from Vietnam. Rory Cook had been shot out of a transport helicopter and dropped nearly a hundred feet. Jack had watched in a horror, compounded by what seemed like slow motion, as his one-time high school teammate was smothered by a mob of North Vietnamese like ants on a grasshopper, as the helicopter desperately withdrew amidst a hail of machine gun fire. Phil Suminsky bled out after stepping on a land mine. Jack had held Phil while watching his friend's still-booted leg twitch three yards away. Combat boots had replaced gridiron cleats worn just a year before.

During his seemingly endless tour, Parson had witnessed and experienced enough to provide fodder for a lifetime's nightmares. Final scenes involving Rory and Phil seemed to have reserved a permanent front row in his nocturnal psyche. And while the night remained the domain of dreams and visions beyond his control, Jack maintained a firm grasp on the day, teaching history and the one PE class in addition to his coaching responsibilities.

Early in the tour, Jack had come to realize that all men needed to cope with this new world and these events for which they were so unprepared. Nothing stateside, including boot camp, had provided any glimpse of the new reality that would meet them in the jungles of Southeast Asia. Constant fire from .50 weapons, whose shells could cut a man in half, followed by weeks of boredom and seemingly endless miles of hiking through open fields in preternatural silence served to eat away at the men, leaving their nerves raw and frayed. Jack determined that the young soldiers around him learned to cope in one of two ways that served to divide them.

The zombies were those who were already dead. They walked, talked, drank, smoked, marched, and fired weapons when the time called for it but had long since given up on returning home. The zombies showed little external fear and seemed resigned to a fate that involved slowly decomposing as their blood and flesh mixed with foreign soil. Few understood why they were there, and even fewer now cared. They no longer wrote home, and Jack had seen some toss unopened mail into bonfires, Kodachrome providing occasional flares of short-lived color as letters and photos turned to ash. While many would die before their tours ended, even more would return to the states, creating a ripple effect of unintended consequences in the decades to come.

Jack tried as best he could to stay away from these dangerous and reckless hulls. Instead, he had clung to the second group of men: men who coped not by making sense of the situation but by simply making it their priority to survive. To a man, these soldiers understood that with each passing minute, hour, day,

28

week, and month the war was inevitably drawing closer to an end. That simple truth served to buoy their every waking thought. While the zombies sought to block out the pain, the survivors relished just enough of it to keep them sharp and vigilant.

Some things could not be avoided, to be sure. Bad luck had pared their ranks on more than one occasion. Short straws, or green officers looking to impress, had drawn dangerous assignments at times. The men knew all too well the cruel reality of friendly fire. Poor strategy and inaccurate mapping had cost lives as well. But the one thing seen time and again was mistakes getting soldiers killed. The survivors would not fall asleep on watch because they were stoned or hung over. They would not wander drunk into the woods to take a leak. They *would* notice tripwires when marching while others were asleep on their feet. Fear could lead to paralysis, it was true, but it was to be befriended, all the same.

Sometimes survivors cracked, surrendering to the ranks of the zombies. Sometimes they got killed despite the exercise of all possible caution. And sometimes they were wounded and sent home where they were given a chance to make good on all the promises they had made to God and themselves regarding the lives they would lead if only given the chance. Such was the case with Jack Parson.

The life Jack had promised to live involved taking over the reins of the football program at Coburn and bettering the lives of the young men under his temporary charge as coach. Jack's father had held onto the job with the hope of handing it to his son upon graduation from a university following Jack's return to the states. Nepotism may have gotten him the job following college, but the younger Parson knew it wouldn't allow him to keep it without producing wins.

The first two seasons under the soldier-turned college boy-turned-coach yielded winning records but first and second round dismissals from the playoffs. Enough to keep Jack secure in the job, but hardly what it took to keep his foremost critic silent. The expectations that Jack Parson had for himself had driven an average athlete to become an all-conference defensive player as well as probably keeping him alive while defending democracy in Southeast Asia.

Parson knew the group he and assistant coach, Elmore Robinson, who had coached for years alongside Jack's father, had coming back next fall had the potential to be something special. Tommy Wilkins was easily the best returning quarterback in the conference; the offense would put up plenty of points, and the defense would hopefully keep them in ball games. Parson also knew the players and coaches at Roseburg High felt the same way, and for good reason, as their star running back was being recruited from coast to coast. The team that emerged from the conference championship would have a chance to go deep into the playoffs. So evenly matched were the teams that each sought something to put them over the top. Parson called that something *the tipping point.*

5

Carlton was sitting at one of the three small outside tables in front of the deli when Trudy walked out after hanging up her apron. The night was clear and warm, a prelude of the summer to come. She looked at the haggard man whose feet were up on another chair as he enjoyed a cigarette and a small glass of beer.

"I thought you didn't smoke," she said, placing his half of the evening's tips on the table in front of him. Her voice was taunting and laced with mockery.

Carlton exhaled toward the sky above before he answered. "One a day, young lady. It's how I end each evening. Care to join me?" he asked quietly.

"Yeah, that's how I want to spend a Friday night. Hot date with Mr. Geritol." She practically spat the words before taking a pink wad of gum from her mouth and tossing it toward the garbage can. The gum fell short of the receptacle, and Trudy looked at Carlton as she pulled her own pack of cigarettes from the bag over her shoulder. He held his lighter toward her, but she ignored the gesture, fishing for her own pink Bic instead. Carlton finally placed his silver lighter on the table and watched as Trudy lit her own cigarette. The smoke that came from her mouth danced blue and gray in the light above her head.

"You've undoubtedly more important things to do," Carlton said softly.

"None more pathetic than you," she responded, before turning and walking away.

Carlton took one last drag and stubbed out his lone cigarette as he watched Trudy turn the corner and disappear from sight. He thought of his own daughter, recalling her at Trudy's age. Ironically, their attitudes and demeanor toward him were not altogether dissimilar, and he wondered how much of it was warranted.

There was resentment in each girl, as if something had been taken from them to which they felt entitled. Carlton knew in the case of his daughter that this was so and wondered what it was that Trudy had lost, sensing that it went deeper than the abandonment she felt from the friend who had moved to Reno without so much as saying goodbye. Perhaps, that *was* the entirety of her loss, Carlton thought. He was acutely aware of what such a loss entailed and shuddered for a moment, despite the warmth of the evening. A shooting star caused him to wonder where his daughter was at that very moment, what she was doing, and if she might be thinking of him. He deemed it unlikely, got up, and went inside before locking up, turning off the lights, and heading up to his studio apartment above the deli.

6

Each spring, teams throughout the state of Pennsylvania were allowed to participate in 'spring drills' for a week after school. Coaches used this week to keep players motivated for the fall, giving the athletes some things to work and think on over the course of the summer if they were both motivated and dedicated. It gave coaches an idea of the numbers and talent they could expect to turn out in the fall. No contact was allowed, just shorts, t-shirts, helmets, and cleats. Agility drills, calisthenics, and pass patterns were all part of the mix, but Coach Jack Parson mostly used the week as a way of lighting a fire under his prospective team. He wanted his squad to taste what was to come and let the underclassmen absorb the attitudes and work habits espoused by the returning players. Also, Parson wanted them all to know that time spent running and in the weight room over the course of the summer would pay dividends come the fourth quarter of most ball games in the fall.

Tommy Wilkins had done his part, as Parson noted Raymond Gaines at the back of the crowd of boys assembled on the field awaiting opening day instruction. The redheaded boy looked both hopeful and uncertain, reminding Parson of the courage it might take for a hearing impaired outsider to try to gain entry into a program most of the other boys had been in since playing Pop Warner as grade schoolers. When the players broke into groups according to position, Raymond remained. Knowing better than to send him with the sure-handed backs and receivers,

Parson flipped through the signed consent forms until he found Gaines'.

"Six-foot-two. Good. I see you left your weight blank, though." Parson smiled, noting the question mark on the form. Raymond shrugged his shoulders sheepishly, and Parson realized the boy likely did not have access to a scale. "That's O.K. I'm guessing about 180 – maybe 185." Parson did the best he could despite Raymond's frame being camouflaged with his usual baggy sweatshirt. Raymond nodded and grinned through teeth that could have yielded a down payment on an orthodontist's sports car.

"Let's send you with the defense, Raymond. It's easier to learn if you're just starting out." Parson made a point of facing Raymond as he spoke so as to give the boy the ability to read his lips. Raymond nodded and loped gracefully over to the group already assembled with assistant coach Robinson in the near end zone.

Coach Robinson grouped the prospective defenders into six lines and instructed them to spread more than an arm's-length apart so they wouldn't be running into one another. He stood at the front of the group and pointed the football he had been holding in one direction. Instantly, the group of defenders broke in the direction he pointed the ball, cross-stepping with haste. The player on Raymond's left crashed into him before he could react. Raymond fell to the ground and waited for others to jeer at his mistake; such had been his experience in the Physical Education class at his former school. Instead, the kid who had knocked him over immediately extended his hand and hastily pulled Raymond to his feet without saying a word. No one else, including Coach Robinson, seemed to notice. When Robinson pointed the ball in the other direction, the entire group, including Raymond, cross-stepped simultaneously in the direction the coach had pointed. The kid on Raymond's left gave him the thumbs up signal as they moved in a synchronized fashion. Robinson pointed toward the players, and Raymond did not need to be told to back-pedal, lowering his center of gravity and pumping his arms aggressively as he saw the other players doing.

That night Raymond had boiled a pan of water and dropped the piece of clear plastic resembling the letter 'U' into the bubbling water. He counted to sixty before fishing the plastic out with a fork and immediately putting it into his mouth and biting down hard, just as Tommy had instructed him to do. He had trusted the quarterback, who promised the hot plastic would not burn his mouth, as metal would have done. After waiting another sixty seconds, Raymond removed the mouth guard and examined the pattern his upper teeth had made. In order to acclimate himself, Raymond kept the guard in his mouth while doing homework that night, guardedly curling his lips over the piece when his father came into the room.

The beginning of practice on Tuesday saw the new players fitted for helmets, as the returning members adjusted the chinstraps on their helmets of the previous season. All the players wrote their names on a strip of athletic tape with a black marker before affixing the strips to the front of their helmets. Raymond's helmet felt strange, heavy, and confining; yet it filled him with pride as he felt a part of something for the first time he could recall. Along with the mouth guard, the helmet linked him with every other player, making him, if in only a small way, like Tommy Wilkins, who, Raymond quickly determined, was clearly the leader of this team numbering several dozen. Coach Robinson introduced the defenders to an obstacle course featuring old tires that the players were expected to high-step through as quickly as possible, a pull-up bar that saw Raymond falter after eight repetitions, and a series of shuttle-runs that were timed with the stopwatch that was ever present around Robinson's neck.

On Wednesday the grizzly old coach instructed Raymond and several other players to retrieve five tackling dummies as well as the large sled from the equipment shed. He demonstrated form tackling, emphasizing safety and warning against spearing that could lead to a neck injury. He paired the teens and had them go through the tackling motion without using real force. Pete Nelson, who had knocked Raymond down on the first day, now gave him tips about wrapping up a ball carrier in order to bring him to the ground. Other players clapped Raymond on the shoulders and repeatedly encouraged him and anyone else who had difficulty.

An hour into Thursday's session, an old, lime green Ford pickup truck parked on the far side of the field, and a man in a dirty and well worn John Deere cap, blue jeans, and greasy t-shirt got out and leaned against the truck's front bumper, arms folded.

Ten minutes later, the overcast sky gave way to light rain. The man didn't budge and continued to stare blankly at the defensive unit as they engaged in a shuttle run. Parson knew most of the player's fathers and could identify those he didn't. This man had to be Raymond's father, and for whatever reason, he didn't look pleased.

Parson glanced at Raymond, who had taken little time in proving he was as fast as any other defender on the team. The kid was demonstrating this speed now and seemed unaware or ambivalent regarding his father's presence across the way. The man, now soaked, remained unmoved as he witnessed the shuttle run. The only change appeared on his face in the form of a hardened glare.

It wasn't until Parson had the entire squad gathered that the man moved. He made a beeline for the team, which was on one knee before Parson, who intended to give them a few words of praise before sending them into the locker room. The man's stride was of determined anger, and Parson instinctively sought to defuse it.

"Good afternoon," the head coach offered in a friendly tone.

The players all turned their attention to the man who was rapidly approaching from behind. Raymond's head was the last to swivel, and he had no time to prepare for the backhand he received from the man. The boy uttered a startled yelp and was helped to his feet as the man grasped a handful of Raymond's red hair and lifted. The startled players all stood and instinctively backed away two steps. It was Parson who moved toward the incident. The man with the John Deere hat held up a ball of fingers with only the index extended.

"You stay out of this," the man barked at the younger coach. And then to Raymond, "You told me you were staying after for school work! This what you call school work?"

Raymond shut his eyes more from humiliation than pain, as if he could wish himself away from any adolescent's worst nightmare. As his face reddened it served to outline the whitened area of the cheek that had received the openhanded blow. Jack Parson's face also reddened, as the response most helpful to Raymond struggled past that which would have served to satisfy Parson personally.

Anything Parson could offer would only serve to ramp the man's distress. So Parson wisely said nothing. The angry man scanned the faces before him and seeing only shock and dismay rather than confrontation, was forced to speak next.

"Get your ass in the truck, boy. I'm going to have a few words with your coach," the man said, emphasizing the last word with disdain. Raymond looked to the truck, his shoulders slumping as he made his way off the field, a far cry from six foot two.

"So tell me, coach. If I refused to sign the damn form, what the hell is my boy doing out here?" Raymond's father spat, stepping close to Parson and tapping the coach on the chest with his still extended index finger.

Such a situation calls for cautious handling. The tattoo Parson was able to glimpse as the man raised his arm made it even more so. The imbedded ink told Parson that he and the man had both spent time in a country doing and seeing things that would forever affect their sleep. The hollow eyes accompanied by a stale beer and cigarette smell made clear to Jack that the common bond had become unspliced in an effort to cope.

Parson held the clipboard, which contained Raymond's signed form, at his side. "I apologize Mr. Gaines. I never should have let Raymond participate without the form. It was a bad judgment call on my part." Coach and father stared eye to bloodshot eye until Gaines looked away.

"Damn right it was," Raymond's father muttered, turning away deflated by Parson's failure to provide resistance.

Parson watched the man stride back to his truck, where his son sat fighting back tears. The coach would no longer wonder if civilian life served to revive the men he had called zombies. The helmet Raymond had worn for the past week looked forlorn sitting in the trampled grass where the team had gathered. Parson stooped and plucked it off the turf by the facemask. Using his thumbnail, Parson peeled the corner of the athletic tape, which simply read 'Gaines.' He was preparing to rip the whole piece off when he thought better of it. A play of words floated into Parson's mind: *Raymond **gains** - by playing football.*

Nearly a week's momentum had been shattered in the space of three minutes, and Parson knew he would have to rebuild as he watched the shaken and disquieted players, head down but already whispering, leave the field. Parson walked toward the equipment shed with Raymond's helmet and a mesh bag full of footballs, leaving his quarterback and assistant coach to bring in a five-gallon water jug.

Each held a side handle and walked in unison. Tommy broke the silence. "I saw the form. How come he didn't show it to Raymond's dad?"

Coach Robinson looked at Tommy and said nothing, waiting for the reader of defenses to make the read. A knowing look on Tommy's face told the seasoned coach when. Robinson then said, as if to himself, "Coach knows the boy's got enough to deal with."

7

Angela Thomas had dealt with Gary Brody's abandonment by taking a box cutter and exorcising her former lover's presence from every photograph she could find in which the man's face was featured. Trudy would have preferred her mother had taken the pictures down, but Angela had always insisted that they remain up and about the home, saying that his disappearance did not mean that the good times portrayed had not taken place. The various pictures featuring her mother, an infantile Trudy, and sometimes Jimmy, or even a few friends had always struck Trudy as creepy, since a jagged hole existed on top of a mysterious body that was tall and fit.

Angela had thrown a fit initially, after discovering the yellow smiley face stickers that Trudy had once placed over all the jagged holes. Jimmy had given his second grade sister a sticker pack he had won at school, and Trudy had put them to good use in a way that she and Jimmy both found amusing. With Jimmy and Trudy both arguing in favor of the smiley faces, Angela eventually relented and even found humor in the array of amended photos.

Before Jimmy had gone to war he had given Trudy an unaltered photo that Angela had snapped and forgotten many years earlier. It featured Gary Brody pushing his daughter on a swing, the toddler holding on tight but shrieking with unmistakable joy. Jimmy had not needed to instruct Trudy on the importance of keeping the picture hidden from their mother. So it was with great care that Trudy removed the photo from a gap behind the faux wood paneling in her closet and examined the picture from time to time.

She might not like it, but Trudy understood why Jimmy and even Rochelle had left. But Trudy would never understand why her father had left her behind. *Hadn't he loved her? How could he just go away and never even call or write? Didn't he wonder how she was doing or what she might look like as she grew older? Did he go on to have other children? If so, would he tell them about her? Or was she just some sort of mistake that he could pretend never happened? What would he say to her if she showed up unannounced on his doorstep one day? Would he shut the door in her face? Or would he welcome her in and introduce Trudy to the new family he had created for himself?* It was something Trudy often imagined: a scenario in which she was not certain what she herself would say, her response differing with her mood at the time.

8

The ride home served to further illustrate the disconnect between father and son. Daniel Gaines' ranting and curses fell, as it were, on deaf ears, for his son stared out of the passenger window, fighting to keep tears from blurring the western Pennsylvania landscape. They were on the road his mother had been on when she had lost control of her vehicle, and Raymond thought of her as he always did when nearing the spot, noted only by the small, green mile marker ten.

Barbara Gaines had consoled her young son for all of two years with stories of his father's bravery in defending the world from the spread of communism, even though Daniel's letters became spaced farther and farther apart until such time as they had stopped coming altogether. Raymond had missed his father terribly and wanted to know all about a war that was so important as to deprive him of his father for month after month. Barbara was often at a loss for words, as she had plied herself with many of these same questions. Instead, she focused on the future and how life would be all the better when Daniel returned. A future she hoped would include a sibling for young Raymond.

A sibling appeared likely as Barbara became pregnant within months of Daniel's return home, but the domestic bliss she had pictured enveloping the reunited family was not to be. Daniel resembled the man she'd married and lived with for five years, in appearance only. Pills, booze, and marijuana had become a staple of his life while overseas, and Daniel showed no inclination toward discontinuation. He showed no interest in finding work and was often inebriated or stoned by noon. Daniel mocked her as she dressed Raymond for church, telling her he had seen proof that God was dead. As bad as were the days, the nights were even worse. Barbara slept lightly, fearing constantly that her husband would strangle her in the throes of one of his nightly torments.

Daniel was deeply troubled and yet refused to speak of his dreams and anguish. Barbara was closed out of what was left of the diminished life he brought back from Vietnam. Daniel was not the same man, father, or lover he'd been before he had left the country. For the sake of Raymond and her unborn child, Barbara refused to give up on her husband, even after Daniel became abusive. On one such occasion, Daniel had stormed out of their trailer, leaving Barbara holding her visibly shaken son, who had seen all, despite hearing little.

Barbara got on her knees and wiping the tears and hair from his face smiled sadly at the boy. He had turned the dial on his hearing aid all the way down so as to drown out the yelling and screaming. She reached gently behind his left ear and adjusted the device. "Your father's not a bad man, Raymond. You remember the way he was before he went to war. He's a good man." Raymond did remember, but daily life with his father was beginning to crowd out the good memories, as Raymond grew increasingly unsettled around the moody and unpredictable man. Always forced to play quietly, so as to not awaken his light-sleeping father, Raymond grew to long for the days when it was just he and his mother.

Barbara rocked her son gently and explained that war had made his father different for a while because of all the bad things he'd seen. It was up to mommy and Raymond and the baby that would be born shortly to remind Daddy of all the good things in life. Barbara promised Raymond that in time his father would return to normal and things would be even better than before. These were words she used to convince them both.

As Raymond looked out the speeding truck's window he wondered if his father would have returned to normal by now if his mother had lived. Raymond closed his eyes and summoned the picture he had etched of her in his mind for over a year now. He had discovered that time had a cruel way of eroding the picture he had previously held of his mother, and Raymond was determined to re-etch daily the mental image he sought to keep.

Raymond's world had been largely silent after his mother's death. It coincided cruelly with the expiration of the battery in one hearing aid, and then the other. Raymond had put the devices in a drawer, not wanting to bother his father with such triviality. In addition to the increasingly necessary skill involved with the reading of lips, Raymond found his ability to concentrate elevated. It was with this concentration that he fondly recalled his mother.

The truck halted at a stop sign, and Raymond looked over at his father who faced him squarely. "I'd like to sue that sorry

S.O.B. for letting you play without my permission. That clown is lucky I didn't kick his ass," Daniel brayed.

Raymond looked away as the truck resumed cruising speed. As he thought of his father harming the first adult to reach out with any modicum of compassion since his mother died, Raymond was seized with a desire to grab hold of the steering wheel and force the truck off the road and into the river in nearly the same location his mother had crashed some ten years earlier.

Then it came to him. Coach Parson hadn't shown his father the signed form. The coach had realized the form had been forged and had not deflected the blame to Raymond. The man had taken the heat in front of the entire team for him, for Raymond Gaines. Sorrow and humiliation melted away as Raymond reflected on the past four days of drills. Of waiting for three o'clock to come so he could insert his mouth guard before dawning shorts, a t-shirt, and a helmet with athletic tape bearing his name across the front. The thrill of the first wind sprints that had defined Raymond as 'having wheels,' the guys all said. Tommy Wilkins had put an arm around him and said that they'd have to find another water boy, indicating that Raymond might actually have the skills to play in a real varsity game. Raymond recalled being on one knee, awaiting words from Coach Parson, while in unison forty other guys breathed deeply, recovering from conditioning drills. There was camaraderie in the locker room that was entirely different from PE class. Parson and many of the returning players spoke of winning games and going to the playoffs. Raymond realized he wanted to taste the concept, as he had never before won anything. All the guys wanted to be there and sought a common result of their unified efforts over the course of a season yet to come.

The elder Gaines cuffed his son on the shoulder. "What are ya grinnin' about ya idiot? You think this is funny?"

The smile disappeared as Raymond looked straight ahead and said evenly, "I want to play."

"You what? You're deaf Raymond. You can't even hear the damn whistle!" His father sneered.

"I want to play," Raymond repeated slightly louder.

"You'd never make the team," his father said.

"They don't cut seniors," countered the son.

"Then you'd never *get* to play," Daniel mocked.

"I don't care. I want to be part of the team," Raymond said, realizing this was the most he and his father had spoken in more than a year.

"No," Daniel Gaines said.

"Why not?" Raymond asked bitterly.

"We'll be clearing the North Slope this fall," Daniel said, putting the matter to rest in his mind.

Raymond was silent. Minutes later he asked, "What if we clear it this summer?"

His father chuckled contemptuously at the thought. "*We* won't."

"Why not?" Raymond demanded.

"'Cause I aint workin' in that heat, Raymond," his father barked.

"I'll do it myself," Raymond said without thinking.

Daniel laughed out loud. "You do that, Raymond," he said, still laughing.

"And if I do?" Raymond persisted.

Father and son came to a halt in front of their trailer. Daniel put the truck in park. He faced his son and smiled sardonically. "Then you can play *cheerleader*, boy."

9

As she approached the mobile home she shared with her
mother and Dirk, Trudy tried to imagine what it would be like to
live in a real home, one with a front lawn and maybe some colorful
flowers lining a driveway. The home she envisioned was not big,
but it was clean, with fresh paint and a wreath on the front door.
Trudy had seen such homes on television, of course, but it was a
home she had been invited to when still in first grade that inspired
her most. It was a time, Trudy now realized, before parents really
had a sense of which children they wanted their own offspring to
befriend. Angela had served to define her daughter's social
parameters that day with an attire that included faux leopard skin
tights, a purple silk shirt unbuttoned at least one notch too many,
and gaudy nails and hair that distracted one nearly to the point
where they missed the faint smell of marijuana, which was
clumsily masked with cheap perfume. It had been the last birthday
party Trudy had been invited to, and while she didn't understand
the causes that day, it had become painfully apparent over time.

The vision of the home she aspired to one day live in
disappeared as Trudy stepped on the rickety wooden block in front
of her mobile home. As she always did before stepping inside,
Trudy held the cool metal of the screen door and took a deep
breath of fresh air. Inside, the mobile home was dimly lit and
smoky, the fresh smoke and smell of marijuana hanging in the air
like transparent pillows. Overnight it would add another layer to
the old smoke, which permeated anything porous and much that

was not, including the fake wood paneling that lined most of the interior walls. With the exception of the cigarette she had lit in a childish effort to show her displeasure with Carlton's hiring, Trudy never smoked indoors and felt strangely stifled by the smoke in her home.

She walked quickly past her mother, who was curled up like a cat next to Dirk on the worn couch. Both were watching an old western on a television that featured a metal clothes hanger in place of the traditional rabbit ears that had long since been broken. A half-dozen empty beer cans and a glass bong sat on a cheap, laminate coffee table alongside Dirk's feet. Two of Dirk's toes were visible through the holes in the thin gray-white socks he wore, and Trudy looked away quickly, the sight somehow as distasteful as the open-chested button-down plaid shirts the man constantly wore, his gold-plated chain glimmering through a forest of graying hair.

"Hey babe," Angela acknowledged her daughter drowsily. Trudy forced a tight-lipped smile in her mother's direction.

"Trudy, grab me a beer. Will ya?" Dirk asked. Despite passing by with haste, Trudy could still feel his eyes on her backside.

"Grab it yourself," Trudy said, as she closed herself inside her small bedroom. It too, was dark but smelled less of smoke than the rest of the home, and Trudy finally exhaled. She took off her backpack, removed a book from inside, and tossed the pack on the bed before kicking off her shoes and putting on her only pair of pajamas. The sheets were cool, and Trudy waited until she was nestled comfortably before reaching for the small light on the nightstand next to her bed. This light allowed her to read *Tale of Two Cities* for the next forty minutes until she closed first the book and then her eyes.

Trudy felt ashamed for the way she had treated the old man her uncle had hired. It had not been the old guy's fault that Rochelle had moved or even failed to say goodbye. Yet, it filled her with resentment, and she had no other way of relieving or even expressing the hurt and disappointment she felt after building up the coming summer into one that would no doubt be a far cry from what she and Rochelle had planned. Turning over on her back, Trudy vowed that she would at least try to be civil to Carlton in the future.

As she always did before falling asleep, Trudy said a prayer for Jimmy. It would have seemed silly or even hypocritical if the prayer had been for her, Trudy reasoned, but since it was for someone else she was all right with the religious implications. Rochelle had declared herself to be an atheist, citing all the problems in the world that a supposedly omnipotent God had sat by and allowed. Trudy, on the other hand was unwilling to say there was no God. She explained to Rochelle that there was too much out there that was unknown, and that she, Trudy, could not make such a determination based on what little she knew and understood. With that in mind, Trudy declared to Rochelle that she was agnostic and therefore open to arguments from either side.

Rochelle had exhaled a raft of cigarette smoke, rolled her eyes, and said as nonchalantly as possible, "Whatever floats your boat, Truds. I don't know why you can't come down on one side or the other, but it's no skin off my back, either way." But Trudy did know why she couldn't land on one side or the other. To acknowledge that there was an all-powerful God meant believing that God had decided Jimmy's life wasn't worth continuing. On the other hand, denying the possibility of God meant Jimmy was nothing, nowhere, and completely gone from existence for all of time. Trudy couldn't bear the thought that Jimmy was nonexistent and preferred to think that he might be in some sort of heaven somewhere.

10

Raymond lay awake until well past midnight thinking about his mother. Like Trudy, Raymond was uncertain as to whether heaven really existed, but he did know that if it did his mother would be among the first in line. Barbara Gaines had fled their home after a prolonged, alcohol-fueled battle with Daniel, who had started early on a rainy Saturday morning, college football blaring as beer cans began piling up on the floor by his chair. By noon Daniel had graduated to distilled spirits, and Barbara instinctively sought to remove Raymond from the scene by taking him to her father's for a visit. Raymond's widowed grandfather lived alone in the midst of a larger, adjoining tract of timber and welcomed his daughter and grandson at all times. Barbara's father had made it clear that Daniel was also welcome, but something had happened between the two that made the son-in-law's appearances few and far between since returning stateside. Daniel saw Barbara instruct Raymond to put on his jacket and asked where they were going. When Barbara explained that she hadn't visited her father in several days, Daniel told her to go, but insisted that Raymond needed to stay.

Daniel explained with words beginning to slur, that a boy needed to learn the game of football from his father, and that college football was a good place to start. Barbara froze. She hadn't expected the resistance since Daniel normally paid so little attention to Raymond, even less when drinking. Pleading with Daniel made him angry, as it made obvious her intent to get

Raymond out of the house and away from his father. Soon Daniel began swearing, a torrent of angry words coming out of his mouth, matched shortly thereafter by reluctant tears spilling from Barbara's eyes. Raymond ran inside his bedroom and closed the flimsy door tightly. He pressed himself against the door as if that might prevent the sounds from penetrating the hollow barrier. The last Raymond heard of the exchange between his parents had been his mother's tearful insistence, "I just don't want Raymond to see you like this." This had been followed by a string of bad words and the sound of a bottle shattering against the potbellied stove. Raymond turned his hearing aid down low and lay on his bed, no longer fighting the tears that had always prompted his father to cuff him on the side of the head and call him soft.

When Raymond awoke it was nearly dark, and rain cascaded in straight lines outside his streaked window. He cracked the door to the bedroom and saw a man with a gold star and insignia on the shoulder of his navy blue jacket talking to Raymond's father. Both men looked very serious, and Daniel's unshaven cheeks held no color whatsoever.

11

The silence of the deli after the thin dinner crowd had passed through allowed Trudy to address homework demands in hopes of not having additional classes added to her summer school schedule. However, the class she was having the most trouble with was also the same subject she was being forced to repeat. Carlton was wiping down tables as Trudy sat at the counter writing in a spiral notebook, a look of bewildered frustration evident on her face.

The look was not lost on Carlton, who asked in a pleasant tone, "What are you writing over there?"

Forgetting her vow of the previous evening, Trudy snapped, "A letter to Charles Manson asking him to father my future children."

This response caused both of Carlton's eyebrows to rise. "Sorry I asked," he said in earnest.

Trudy softened. "I'm sorry. It's just that this assignment is so stupid."

Carlton straightened. "Maybe I can help."

"I doubt it." Trudy erased a dozen words with an eraser that was nearly spent.

Carlton shrugged and picked up the rag he had been using to wipe the tables. "You might be surprised," he said quietly.

Trudy wrinkled her nose as she looked at her paper. "I mean, how can it be the best of times and the worst of times at the same time?"

A knowing look came over Carlton's face. "It was the age of wisdom, it was the age of foolishness, it was the epoch of belief, it was the epoch of incredulity," he recited in a way that reminded Trudy of the way actors on stage spoke in a play she had seen performed at her high school the previous year.

Trudy opened the Dickens novel on the counter and turned to the first page while Carlton continued, "It was the season of light, it was the season of darkness…"

"Got it. Thanks," she said, suppressing a smile. "You read the book. Now what's it mean?"

Carlton tossed the dirty rag into the sink and wiped his palms on his apron. "I suspect Dickens was referring to varying perspectives," he said.

"What do you mean?" Trudy asked, wrinkling her nose again.

"What does this job mean to you, Trudy?" Carlton responded.

Trudy thought for a moment, wary that it was some kind of trick question. She considered telling Carlton of the car she wanted to buy, but once again thought better of it. "I don't know. School clothes. Money to do things with my friends," she said, wondering if the old man could sense that she no longer had any of the latter.

Without pause, Carlton replied, "And yet, this very same job, in conjunction with my meager social security, allows me to subsist." He then grabbed a broom from a small closet and began to sweep the floor. Trudy watched as he swept the fading linoleum with gentle, rhythmic passes. For some reason it reminded her of a couple dancing, the entire dance floor to themselves, oblivious of all else.

12

After devouring the contents of a can of chili smothering three pieces of stale bread the following morning, Raymond pocketed four small apples in his sweatshirt and stepped out of the dilapidated trailer. He walked the short distance to what his father referred to as the North Slope.

The North Slope was, in fact, the forty-acre tract of white pine and hemlock that sloped down to a small creek behind the trailer. It was land that his grandfather had left to Raymond's mother in his will. His mother had never possessed the land, as she had predeceased her father by just months, leaving Daniel Gaines with stewardship over the land until Raymond turned eighteen years of age, at which point the timber-rich land was to become legally his: this unbeknownst to the boy, since Daniel had never seen fit to explain the arrangement to his son. Harvesting and reaping the proceeds were the sole reasons for Daniel's return to Coburn, and in a twist of cruel irony he intended to use his unwitting son to perform the bulk of the task - a task that would effectively transfer Raymond's future into his father's present.

Daniel's opposition to Raymond's playing football was threefold. Football would take Raymond away from the work at hand. Fall was the time after the oppressive heat diminished and before the snows came. Additionally, an injury to Raymond could leave Daniel the lion's share of the work. But another deep-seated reason lurked in the back of Daniel Gaines' mind. He was ashamed of the boy, born with fiery red hair, who resembled neither his mother nor father. Hearing impaired and hard to understand, Raymond had been labeled as slow in school despite his mother's insistence that her son was quite bright. The first of two growth spurts had left Raymond ungainly and awkward, his coordination still playing catch-up all through his junior year. Gangly and clumsy were hardly the makings of a skilled football player. For Daniel, it had been bad enough being the star of a team that had won only four games. Raymond's inevitable failure would only serve to cement his father's ignominy.

The forty-acre tract of mixed pine and hemlock was anomalous among the thousands of acres of rolling scrub and brush. Early in the century the surrounding forests had been cleared following the widespread logging on both sides of the Ohio River. The uneven land would hold little value and even less beauty after the lumber left on a string of trucks, bound for mills near Pittsburgh, the pine to be used for the making of trusses, the hemlock in a myriad of other uses.

Raymond stared into the woods he had come to for solace since moving back to Coburn. Birds flew from tree to tree as a gentle breeze washed over the slope. It was with sadness that he realized these tranquil trees were what stood between him and what he now wanted most in the world. The following afternoon would not be spent doing drills in preparation for fall football, but Raymond would be laying the groundwork, all the same.

13

As Trudy had seen so many times before, Mr. Renton helped Mrs. Renton out of her chair and placed her coat over her shoulders after both had finished eating their customary meals. Trudy watched as the man patiently held the door for his wife. More than once, while watching the elderly couple, Trudy had wondered if she would someday marry such a man, one like Mr. Renton, who seemed to worship the very ground on which his wife stood. Were any such men still in existence? Was such chivalry still being taught to sons that would carry out such tender devotion to young women who would become wives and eventually mothers to their children?

Trudy left her spiral notebook open on the counter as she went to clear the Renton's table. After doing so, she resumed her work on the paper while Carlton washed the dishes she had cleared.

"How's your paper coming?" Carlton asked twice before Trudy heard him.

"Just dandy," she said, disturbed that her train of thought had been broken once again. Almost immediately she recalled her vow to be kinder and wondered how flippant her response had sounded to Carlton, who continued with the dishes. Before she could follow up, a family of four entered the diner. Trudy begrudgingly got off her stool, rolled her eyes, and grabbed four menus from the wood-slatted box at the end of the counter. "God," she mumbled under her breath, "I'm never going to get this stupid paper done."

Fifteen minutes later, Trudy was bringing the family their entrees when a tall, lean, teenage boy walked into the deli. He wore a leather bomber jacket and had black hair slicked back in the way that was popular two decades earlier. The teen sat at a small table in the corner by the window and put a sneakered foot up on an adjacent chair before pulling a toothpick out of his mouth. After bringing Ketchup and mustard to the family's table, Trudy brought the boy a menu.

Noticing that Trudy was soon engaged in flirtatious conversation with the boy, Carlton stood at the counter and peered at his co-worker's open spiral notebook. Soon, he was as engrossed in the paper Trudy was writing as she was in the leather-bound youth.

Long after the family of four departed, the teenager and Trudy sat talking quietly in the corner. The kid had devoured a burger, shake, and two helpings of fries but remained, flashing a toothy grin at Trudy in a way that caused her to blush more than once. Carlton had scrubbed the grill, done the dishes, refilled the salt and napkin dispensers, and was mopping the floor by the time the tall boy finally zipped up his jacket and got up from the table.

"I've got to go," he said, as if pressed for time. He tilted his head back in a self-assured fashion, telling Trudy, "Maybe I'll see you around."

Trudy blushed again. "Maybe," she said in a voice Carlton had never heard before. "I'm stuck here all summer, Bobby."

Bobby sauntered out the door. Carlton watched Trudy, who was watching Bobby, who was watching himself in the reflection of the plate glass windows in the front of the deli. When Trudy finally turned around she saw Carlton gaping at her. "Why don't you take a picture? It'll last longer," she snarled, recalling Rochelle having uttered the snappy quip months earlier.

14

Parson noted Raymond in line the following Monday as he took roll call. The youth hung his red head low but managed to say "here" when his name was called. Reasoning that Raymond had kept one eye on the kid to his left who preceded him alphabetically, Parson wondered at the many tricks Raymond had undoubtedly learned along the way. It occurred to the coach that Raymond must have learned and developed many such techniques in order to adapt to a soundless world. The boy was likely far brighter than most would give him credit for being, Parson surmised. The harmonious sounds of his daughter's Christmas concert just months earlier came to mind, and Parson winced as he recalled the ugly contrasting scene involving Raymond's father the previous week.

Little else had occupied Jack Parson's mind over the weekend. He had contemplated paying Daniel Gaines a visit, trying to reason with the man one-on-one. Maybe, once Gaines realized their common bond as former soldiers, the man would soften and allow Raymond to partake in something in which his father had once excelled. Robinson had informed Parson that Daniel Gaines had been a star receiver on one of the few mediocre teams Jack's father had fielded when the future coach was still a kid. The talented receiver had been good enough to attend NC State on a scholarship, according to Robinson. It somehow saddened Parson to hear Robinson describe Daniel Gaines as having been a neat kid with a lot of potential. Both coaches had sat in their office shaking their heads and wondering about how much potential had been wrung out of an entire generation of young men.

Parson knew that paying a visit to Raymond's father could also backfire, and he wondered at the possible repercussions. The last thing Jack wanted to do was to make things tougher on the younger Gaines. In the end, he decided to give the situation more time to cool off; maybe drop in to visit the man at the end of the school year, or better yet, run into him in town where he could offer to buy Daniel a cup of coffee. Either way, Jack reasoned, the man needed some time to cool off after last week's blow-up.

So it came as a surprise when after class Raymond rapped his knuckles tentatively on the window of Jack's office and handed him a note after being waved in. At first glance it appeared to be merely a note excusing Raymond for missing class the previous Friday. Parson nodded to Raymond, acknowledging that the absence would be marked as excused. He was struggling to come up with something to assuage Raymond's humiliation from their last encounter, but the boy turned and left before Parson could summon the words. Parson began to crumple the note when he noticed writing on the other side. The writing was of the same hand that had signed Raymond's spring football permission form. It indicated that Raymond had struck a deal with his father allowing him to play football in the fall. Included in the note were both thanks and an apology regarding the forged permission form. It was signed 'Raymond Gaines.'

Parson was left to wonder what kind of deal had been struck. Daniel Gaines had not left the coach with the impression that he was an easy man with which to deal.

15

Trudy emerged from the warmth of the deli to a light misting. She found Carlton in his customary chair at the outside table nearest the entrance. He was enjoying his lone smoke of the day while petting a stray with a pronounced limp. The dog was a mutt with an obvious Labrador lineage. It was quite lean, its ribs were visible, and its light colored coat badly matted as if it had rolled in a pot of honey or glue. Carlton smiled at Trudy warmly as she wrinkled her nose at the mangy dog.

"Later," was all Trudy said before turning her back and walking in the direction of home.

"You know," Carlton said before Trudy had gotten halfway down the block. "There's more to you than an angry brat who puts her makeup on in the dark."

Trudy stopped in her tracks and whirled around until she faced Carlton. She stood in a shaft of light, which cast her pale face so that her complexion appeared even whiter than normal in contrast to the dark lipstick and heavy black mascara surrounding her eyes. "What the hell is that supposed to mean?" she asked, her ire having quickly risen to the surface.

Carlton exhaled, the smoke rising like a blue wreath above his head. He too, was visible in the warm light from the deli at his back. "I mean you're talented."

In no mood to be trifled with, Trudy put a hand on her hip. Her book-laden shoulder bag slipped and fell to her wrist, jarring her defiant pose. She ignored the bag and fixed her glare on the old man. "What are you talking about?"

"I think you're a gifted writer," Carlton said quietly.

"How would you kn-" She stopped. "You read my paper?" Trudy asked in disbelief.

"You have real-," Carlton began.

"You had no right!" Trudy stomped on the sidewalk like a petulant child. Tears that had always seemed to remain close to the surface welled up in her eyes, and she balled her hands into fists. "You had no right!" she repeated with even greater vehemence than before.

The teenage girl's reaction caught Carlton off guard. It wasn't, he had reasoned, like he was reading her diary or anything of a personal nature. That wasn't something he would have even considered. "I'm sorry. It was just lying there, open on the counter," he attempted to explain.

Tears broke like a dam giving way as Trudy screamed at Carlton, who had reddened deeply at seeing the distress he had caused his young co-worker. "You're so pathetic!" Trudy screamed, as a lifetime of bitterness and frustration overwhelmed her. "You were such a loser during your lifetime that you have to work during your old age, when you should be playing with your grandkids or whatever else old people do!"

Leaning back in the wire chair, more than a little deflated, Carlton nodded. "I do. It's true."

Seeing that he offered no real resistance to her rage only served to heighten Trudy's angst. "God, I hate you, old man!" she stomped again as mascara trailed toward her chin. And then she shrieked something she could never before have imagined saying to another person. "Why don't you just go somewhere and die?" With that, Trudy shouldered her bag and walked away with clipped, angry strides.

Exhaling, Carlton sighed deeply. "In due time," he said to himself. "God willing." The dog at his feet nuzzled Carlton's hand as if sensing the man's woe. Carlton scratched behind the dog's ears and smiled weakly. Suddenly, he felt old and very tired. He reached for his cigarette pack on the table with the thought of breaking his ritual and having another. But as he did so it began to rain in earnest. Carlton glanced toward the heavens, raised a suspicious eyebrow, and rose, retiring the pack to his shirt pocket as he stood.

"Come on," Carlton said to the mongrel as he opened the door to the deli. "The rain's no place for a couple of old strays like us."

16

Parson's supposition that Raymond was far brighter than most people realized was truer than even he would have suspected. For Raymond had calculated in his head and then on paper with astounding accuracy the number of trees on the North Slope. After learning the area inside a single square acre from a table in the back of his math book, Raymond walked off such a parcel of land and counted the trees inside the confines of the acre in question. Using a formula not altogether unlike that which might be used by lumber brokering professionals in determining board feet, Raymond concluded that if he were to work at such and such a rate through not only the summer but the remainder of spring, he and his father would be able to clear the North Slope in time for Raymond to participate in football come the fall. Raymond would do the physically demanding work involved with the felling and quartering of the trees, leaving Daniel with the far less taxing forklift operating when the time came. Any number of variables could throw Raymond's calculations off, and he had little or no margin of error, but the inspired youth clung to the mathematics that suggested his goal was indeed possible.

Mingling with these thoughts as Raymond drifted off to sleep was the warm feeling he got recalling the spring workouts before his father had shown up at the field of practice. The players always helped one another off of the ground, even when on opposing sides of the ball. They cheered each other when doing drills, encouraging greater effort and always in a positive tone.

The high-fiving and backslapping was not something Raymond had witnessed or participated in before, and he had winced the first few times someone had clapped him on the shoulder. In time, even his helmet and mouth guard had grown comfortable and begun to feel a part of him. As much as Raymond had grown to admire Tommy Wilkins, who seemed to pay him special attention in terms of explaining rules and offering tips on technique, it was Coach Parson who had made the greatest impression on the hearing impaired young man. Raymond could still not believe that the coach, who barely knew Raymond, had taken the brunt of his father's wrath in order to shield a deaf, first-year player who couldn't even catch a football.

The last of the thoughts that played through Raymond's drowsy mind was a nascent hope that his father would somehow change when he saw just how important being part of the team was to his son. Raymond pictured working alongside the man, the North Slope clearing gradually as his father began to thaw. Maybe spending time together was what Daniel Gaines needed in order to regain an understanding of what was important in this life far from Southeast Asia and whatever it was overseas that had changed him from the loving father he once was.

17

Carlton looked up from the newspaper he was reading on the counter of the empty deli when Trudy walked in wearing her Army jacket and backpack. She avoided eye contact with the man as she walked past him and into the kitchen. Three minutes later, she emerged while tying her apron behind her back. "I'm sorry," she declared softly.

Once more, Carlton looked up from his paper. "For what are you sorry?" he asked.

Trudy looked him in the eyes. "For being such a bitch last night. You didn't deserve that."

Carlton creased the newspaper and furrowed his brow. He seemed to contemplate Trudy's words for a minute before he said, "I don't know about women, but for a man, apologizing seems to be the hardest thing. The ability to do so suggests character, I suspect."

Trudy nodded awkwardly and began to organize the menus as an uneasy truce hung in the air.

The evening shift had been unusually busy, placing any residual tension squarely on the back burner as Carlton and Trudy struggled to keep up with the orders in addition to clearing, cooking, and cash registering. As they divvied up the evening's tips on the table outside, Trudy commented that while the shift had been no day at the beach, at least the tips were good.

Carlton gave her a tight-lipped smile. "What? You don't like the beach?" Trudy asked.

"Not especially," Carlton commented. Trudy was about to inquire as to why not when Carlton asked, "Have you ever been to the beach, Trudy?"

"Once," she reflected. "How come you don't like-"

"Tell me about it," Carlton interrupted her.

"It was a long time ago," Trudy said. Carlton smiled, and Trudy realized a long time ago to Carlton likely meant decades before she was even born. "Okay, maybe not so long ago," she corrected herself. "I was probably seven or eight."

"Go on," Carlton prompted her.

Trudy hesitated, unsure she wanted to share the experiences of that particular day with a man she hardly knew. But suddenly, Trudy wanted to relive and recapture even part of a day she thought about more than she would normally allow herself to admit. She had never talked about it before, even with Rochelle, but sensed she could recollect it better through words than mere thoughts, in the same way that a flower smells more vibrant when the air is warm as opposed to cold.

"It was before my brother, Jimmy, left home," Trudy began. She would not tell this man where Jimmy had gone. Telling Carlton about the day at the beach was more than she had planned: she would not tell him about losing Jimmy, too. "My mom woke us up, which was strange because I usually had to wake her and Jimmy up. She was in a great mood, dancing around, talking about what a beautiful day it was. And it was. The kind of day where a t-shirt and shorts is all you need. Like the smart alec he was, Jimmy said if it was such a nice day, then why didn't mom let us skip school so we could all go to the beach. For once, my mom was able to shut Jimmy's big mouth, because she just looked at him and said, 'Pack a bag, kids. We're going to the beach.'"

Carlton cracked a smile. "And you went."

"Yeah," Trudy was smiling as well. "We drove all morning. Got there and had lunch. It was colder than at home, but we didn't care. We played in the sand. Waded up to our knees in the freezing cold water. Jimmy and I built a giant hand in the sand. He wanted it to do the middle finger, but my mom wouldn't let him," Trudy mused. "We didn't get home until after dark. And then we realized we all had sunburns."

"Other than the sunburns, it sounds like a wonderful experience," Carlton commented.

Trudy's expression changed, as if she had just come back from the moment. "Yeah," she said. "It was. It was almost like we were a normal, happy family."

It was quiet as both Trudy and Carlton took drags from their cigarettes. "Hey, you never answered my question," Trudy said suddenly.

"What question was that?"

"How come you don't like the beach?" she asked. "You get sunburnt, too?"

"Sunburnt? Yes, in addition to almost drowning the only time I went," Carlton replied without hesitation. He then ground out his half-smoked cigarette and got up before Trudy could respond. "It's been a long day, Trudy."

18

School became more enjoyable as Raymond found he had a teammate or two in most classes. These other boys never made reference to the incident that had so marred the week of spring practices. There were times when Raymond was tempted to believe the ugliness had never taken place. The camaraderie that was felt on the practice field somehow extended to the classroom and even cafeteria as Raymond became accepted in both. He rarely spoke but basked in a level of acceptance for which he suspected he had Tommy Wilkins to thank.

Girls who had once appeared leery around Raymond soon relaxed when Tommy put his arm around the fiery-haired, freckled boy and spoke admiringly of his blazing speed. The girls were pretty, and while it was beyond Raymond's wildest dreams that any of them would take an interest in him, he enjoyed their presence all the same. Forgetting that the loss of a sense can serve to heighten those that remained, Raymond would inhale through his nose and enjoy the scent of strawberry or apricot shampoos all around him.

As the spring matured, both Raymond and his father fell into a familiar pattern. Upon his return from school, Raymond would mix oil and fuel following the ingestion of as many calories as he could muster. He would sit on the trailer's porch using a round file to work away the burrs on the cumbersome saw's chain in the light of the late afternoon sun, while his father sat in a lawn chair, nursing forty ounces of cold malt liquor that was never in danger of growing warm. Daniel would chuckle to himself as he watched the boy, as if in possession of knowledge beyond Raymond's understanding. The older Gaines would sit on the porch until dusk, listening for the creak of the next tree to surrender to the ungodly combination of steel, the combustible engine, and gravity. The tall trees would crash to the ground often taking branches from neighboring trees, as though they were desperate reachings of some sort.

The boy's foolish resolve had Daniel doing some mental math of his own as May wound to a close. He had expected Raymond to give up after a week or so, but the boy showed no signs of weakening and seemed to thrive as additional daylight extended his daily window of work. With Daniel's help and any moderation in summer temperatures, it became conceivable that the task *could* be accomplished by September. However, while the felling of trees could be accomplished by a determined individual, Daniel well knew, the loading of logs onto the flatbed was strictly a two-man operation. Daniel couldn't help but to smile as he clinked the flatbed's keys against a nearly empty beer bottle.

19

The routine that Trudy and Carlton found themselves enmeshed involved Carlton doing the dishes and cleaning the kitchen after the evening diners left, while Trudy sat and watched Bobby Jasper gorge himself on a sandwich or burger and milkshake that Trudy made specially for her new boyfriend each evening. Carlton bit his tongue and bided his time as he watched Trudy gush at every little thing Bobby said. The oddly paired co-workers had agreed to balance the workload, with Trudy taking care of the floor and tables after Bobby left. From time to time a diner or two would straggle in. Trudy would manage to tear herself away from Bobby long enough to take an order and bring it to Carlton, who would then prepare it so that Trudy could reluctantly deliver it to the table in question.

On one such occasion two bubbly teenage girls entered the deli. After taking their order, Trudy told Carlton she would make the BLTs that had been ordered. It soon became apparent that Trudy was making Bobby one as well. Carlton kept quiet and sat on a stool behind the counter, taking weight off his aching feet and back. He pretended to read while noticing the eye contact Bobby was making with one of the girls who was facing in the teen's direction. The girl, wearing a tight, pink cashmere sweater and matching lip gloss, clearly welcomed the attention from the rakish teen in leather, his feet propped up with a cavalier demeanor that suggested he owned the place.

Bobby winked at the girl as Trudy, with her back turned, set the sandwiches on the table in front of the loquacious pair. To Carlton, the kid appeared less than grateful when Trudy delivered his BLT. Within minutes of wolfishly devouring the sandwich, Bobby got up to leave. Trudy followed him out the door and kissed her surly boyfriend goodnight. He held on to her, prolonging the kiss. She did not seem to mind until he groped her chest with his hand causing Trudy to squirm uncomfortably and look out the corner of her eye to see if any of the patrons inside the deli were watching. Before long, Bobby slapped her on the bottom, laughing as she scurried inside while straightening her apron.

The next night Carlton waited until Trudy had finished the floor and tables before engaging in his evening smoke. While he waited, Carlton worked on the coat of the dog he and Trudy had dubbed Roscoe, because it had been the first thing out of the girl's mouth when Carlton had asked for a suggestion. The dog's ribs had become less visible, and every evening Carlton had made a bit of progress on Roscoe's coat. Whatever had been plastered to the poor animal was slowly yielding to a stiff brush and the measured snips from a pair of scissors Carlton had acquired at a nearby pet shop.

When Trudy finally came through the door she was putting an arm through one of the straps to her backpack while holding a small box designated for leftovers in the other hand. Bobby had failed to make his nearly nightly appearance at the deli, and Trudy had been strangely quiet all evening.

Carlton offered Trudy a cigarette from his pack. She put it in her mouth, and he stood and lit both of their cigarettes. "I hate to break our workable truce," he said uneasily.

"Then don't," Trudy responded with a guarded tone.

Carlton exhaled above his head. "Can't help myself."

"Okay. So spit it out," Trudy said coldly, bracing for whatever Carlton was about to say.

"Sit down for a second." Carlton gestured, as he sank slowly back into his chair in front of the table nearest the door.

Trudy reluctantly followed suit. "What's on your mind?" she asked.

"Fellow you're taking the sandwich to is no good," Carlton said, biting his lower lip.

Trudy's spine stiffened, and she gave Carlton an icy stare. "And you know this how?"

"Just do," Carlton said, touching his finger to the tip of his tongue and removing a fleck of tobacco. "The mangy cur will cheat on you first chance he gets." Trudy froze, a moist film appearing over her eyes as Carlton continued. "He's just using you for the food." Carlton looked away as he finished, "and whatever else he can get from you."

Trudy stood, and as she did tears broke from the corner of each eye. "Because no guy could like me for me," she finally said. "Is that it?"

"I didn't say that." Carlton shook his head.

Trudy backed away, creating space between them. "What makes you such an expert? Have you ever been married?" she asked with vitriol.

Carlton nodded slowly. "And divorced," he admitted.

Trudy laughed cruelly. "I rest my case," she spat.

"Fair enough." Carlton said, still nodding. "Just watch yourself with that fellow. You're better than that."

20

On the last day of school Raymond waited in line to turn in his phys. ed. gear. He noticed Coach Parson handing all the guys who had attended spring drills pieces of blue paper from a stack on the counter. Raymond handed the coach his gear and was both relieved and grateful when Parson held out one of the blue flyers for him to take. "See you in August, Raymond," the coach said, looking him in the eye and smiling confidently. It occurred to Parson that he had shortchanged Raymond, who was now wearing a T-shirt, by at least ten pounds two months earlier.

Raymond could only grin and nod before moving out of the line. He grasped the paper with two hands as if afraid a wind might take it away. The paper, which read, DAILY DOUBLES at the top, was a schedule of two-a-day practices beginning in the third week in August. Raymond's heart sank as he chided himself for failing to realize that practice started well before school commenced. August. It was with September and the beginning of school in mind that Raymond had broken down the task at hand, plotting progress points along the way, always factoring optimistically. A deadline of August nineteenth necessitated either an extension from his father or a greater contribution in terms of effort from the man. Neither seemed likely.

21

Rochelle and Carlton's voices intermittently played inside Trudy's head as she and Bobby engaged in heavy petting in a car he had borrowed from a friend. It was clear why Bobby had borrowed the car; Trudy would never bring him or any other boy to her home, and Bobby said his brothers were always present at his house. Rochelle had always spoken casually about sex, and it was clear to Trudy that her friend viewed it as a means to an end or even a negotiating chip when dealing with boys. This was likely consistent with her own mother's view, as Trudy could remember finding different men sitting in their underwear eating her dry cereal on mornings when Angela finally emerged from her bedroom, hungover and similarly clad.

But to Trudy, sex had to be more meaningful than a card to be played and ultimately cheapened. The act was too intimate; it made one too vulnerable to be viewed as little more than an activity to engage in without a serious level of commitment and love. Trudy had never said as much to Rochelle, had always claimed the boys they knew in school were punks, but the truth was that Trudy was saving herself. The concept somehow seemed in tandem with Carlton's last words to Trudy, *You're better than that.*

Bobby acted callous and uncaring when Trudy pulled away and smoothed her rumpled cotton blouse. "I'm not ready," she had said.

"Yes you are," Bobby responded, as if he were in possession of some sort of gauge or barometer that determined the readiness of virgins of all stripes.

"No. I'm *not*," Trudy had said firmly.

Bobby had turned the car's ignition in disgust. "Whatever," he muttered as he put the borrowed vehicle in drive. It was silent as he drove her home, and he did not kiss Trudy goodnight, saying only, "I can't wait forever, Trudy."

22

The crack of dawn the following day saw Raymond
polishing off a square of stale cornbread. He rose from the front
porch and fired up the chainsaw as he walked the well-worn path
toward the section of trees that yet remained vertical. They came
crashing to earth in rapid succession as Raymond worked his way
systematically and with renewed purpose through the dwindling
trees for the next five days. At the end of the fifth day he trudged
up the dusty hill as the sun was setting and turned around to gaze at
the carnage of his making. It was the look given by many a farm
boy who had made the mistake of getting attached to a pig or calf
he'd fed and watered day after day, despite warnings from those
who knew better. The trees had had to come down. If sacrifice
had to be made, let something good come from it, Raymond once
again reasoned as he realized the easy part was now complete.

"They're all down," Raymond said, as he wearily set the
still-warm chainsaw down on the porch in front of his father.

Daniel sniffed the pungent oil that lingered in the air and
spat out of the side of his mouth as if purging his palate of
something distasteful. "So?" he said, twisting the cap from a bottle
of beer that he removed from the Styrofoam cooler at his side.

"So the lumber is ready to be hauled out of there,"
Raymond said, treading carefully, sensing his father's displeasure.

"Yeah? Well, I'm ready to go fishing tomorrow," Daniel
declared, snapping the bottle cap from his fingers. The cap

bounced off Raymond's chest and settled in the dust at his feet. "Wanna go?"

Raymond had known that the time would come when he would need his father's help. He had hoped that his father would relent and somehow be proud of how hard Raymond had worked every evening and weekend, convinced that if it was this important to Raymond that it should somehow matter to him. Raymond had continuously reminded himself of his mother's belief that her husband could be brought around, that there was a good and decent man still within his father's shell. If this was so, Raymond realized, that man wouldn't be reached tonight, and he merely replied, "No thanks," before walking past his father and into the trailer.

As Daniel's renewed penchant for fishing extended beyond a week, Raymond felt his goal slipping away. Still, the operation was not brought to a standstill. Raymond busied himself with stripping limbs and cutting the trees into transportable links. But the optimally cool June mornings were waning, and he knew his father would be even less inclined to work as the oppressive heat of July and August came on in stifling waves.

It is unknowable how long Daniel would have continued filling coolers with beer and bait. Unfortunately for Raymond, he could only wait and hope for his father's mind to change. As it turned out, it was Daniel's own misfortune that changed his muddled mind. Getting cleaned out in a poker game in town served to revive Daniel's interest in hauling the logs up to where they could be loaded onto tractor-trailers and taken to the mill for sale. So diametric were their interests, that Raymond's hopes were buoyed by his father's consistent failure to produce better than a pair of tens.

Despite communication that was both sparse and terse, father and son worked well together in loading the twenty-plus foot sections of white pine onto the flatbed. A sober Daniel demonstrated considerable skill with the old John Deere equipped as a forklift. Guiding and securing the logs on the truck with great care was Raymond's job, and he did it deftly, signaling his father with his hands to facilitate placement.

The distance between them was most evident at lunchtime when Daniel sat on a log and smoked after eating a bologna sandwich. Under different circumstances it would have provided father and son with a natural time and setting to talk about any number of subjects, many of which would have allowed a father to impart wisdom, values, or ideals to a son who would be making his own way in the world before long. The circumstances being what they were, though, Raymond worked through lunch, stripping branches and sizing logs in an effort to stay a day ahead of the loading. He would not allow himself to be the cause of even a moment's work stoppage.

Raymond watched as the last of the big trucks took the remainder of the white pine away. He knew that the check his father had just received, in conjunction with the July heat, would likely suspend the man's participation until cooler fall weather approached. In anticipation of his father's hiatus, Raymond planned to cut the hemlock into smaller sections, enabling him to load them by himself. It would take more time, to be sure, but it was the only way Raymond could imagine bringing the lumber to the loading zone on his own.

Sure enough, the only thing to get between Daniel Gaines and the liquor store had been a trip to the bank, the former facilitating the latter. The distant and intermittent revving of the chainsaw on the slope behind him served to annoy the man as he sought solace in the sipping of aged and iced eighty proof. *Why couldn't the boy just leave it alone? Take a break for a single evening. Give it a damn rest, for once.*

There had been moments when the man Barbara Gaines had once known and loved came close to resurfacing. Daniel had noted with bitterness the irony that had his wife, every bit a survivor, succumbing to death, while he, who had given up readily, trudged on, marking his days by adding crushed glass to a rusty burn barrel that smelled of sour mash.

The late spring and early summer evenings in which Daniel had sat in his lawn chair listening to the distant sounds produced by his son's labors had inspired an almost curious but detached study of the boy. No longer able to feel or attach meaning to a cause, Daniel had noted his son's intense and consuming desire to be a part of a team. What little they had in common would vanish, as Raymond sought inclusion in a society that Daniel had all but forsaken.

Despite the whisky's warm glow evolving into a mind-muddling morass, Daniel recognized the boy's plan. The sound he was now hearing was the downsizing of logs that would enable Raymond to continue the project without his father's help. It was a passive-aggressive form of defiance, a repudiation of Daniel's will. It was a declaration that said, *you cannot stop me - don't even try.*

Whisky has a curious effect on some men. Many will turn sentimental, maudlin, or nostalgic, while others become violent, mean, and unfeeling. Replacing cheap malt and hops with rye whisky revealed Daniel Gaines to be of the latter variety and enabled him to suppress any influence his former self might have had on the man who had returned from Vietnam. As his mind became murkier one thing became clearer. Raymond *would* not, *could* not, finish clearing the land in time to play football.

23

The piercing glances Trudy cast Carlton's way did not go unnoticed, but he did not acknowledge them, either. In silence, the pair readied the deli for nine o'clock when they would open for brunch. A lengthy caravan of colorful vans and trucks made its way by on the street, passing in front of the deli windows.

"Big doings," Carlton observed, breaking the silence.

"Carnival," Trudy replied tersely. "Comes to town every Fourth of July."

"You going?" Carlton ventured.

"With my ever-so-faithful boyfriend," Trudy mocked.

"Yeah, about that," Carlton said.

Trudy turned and faced the man that had disparaged her first love. "What about him?"

"Look, Trudy," Carlton began. "I just don't want to see you get hurt, is all."

"And why would I get hurt?" Trudy asked.

"I know how young men think, Trudy," Carlton said. "I know what they want."

"And what exactly do they want?" Trudy dared Carlton to say what he was implying.

"Most of them want to separate you from your virtue," Carlton said, his eyes on the floor between them.

"What exactly is that supposed to mean?" Trudy reddened as Carlton's meaning not only occurred to her but reminded her of something Rochelle might have said, although in jest.

"You know what I mean. He's a rake. Your young fellow has only one thing on his mind," Carlton said quietly.

"That's not true," Trudy said. She wondered if her words sounded as hollow as they felt. A voice inside Trudy's head chided her, saying, *two things, actually: sex AND food.*

"Okay," Carlton said, ringing his hands. "You know this Mr. Jasper far better than I do. But, I can tell you this. A gentleman does not paw a young woman for whom he regards with respect and admiration the way that rascal was pawing you in front of your uncle's deli," Carlton said, pointing out the window where Bobby had practically mauled Trudy a week before.

Trudy's blush deepened, and it was now she who averted her eyes. "What Bobby and I do is our business," she said in a dour tone.

"Fair enough," Carlton conceded. He had been tempted to say it was everyone's business if they conducted *theirs* in public, but he let it go. "Enjoy the carnival. I'm sure you'll have fun."

"*We* will, I'm sure," Trudy, still mad, shot back. "And what earth-shattering plans have *you* made for the evening?"

Carlton appeared to think for a moment before replying, "I think I'll have a small glass of beer and a smoke outside."

Trudy stifled a bitter laugh. "And that's different from every other night, how?" she asked with cruel mirth.

"Presumably the sky will be laced with fireworks," Carlton replied off the top of his head.

"Very exciting, I'm sure," Trudy said sarcastically.

"Simple pleasures, my dear. Simple pleasures," was all Carlton said by way of reply.

24

The Fourth of July arrived and with it an embellished sense of bitterness in a man who had forfeited so much of his soul for his country. Nonetheless, veteran Daniel Gaines settled into his lawn chair well before noon, certain of fireworks well before dark. He would not be disappointed, as Raymond soon came storming up the slope and around the trailer, his face and hair of similar hue.

"The tractor won't start," Raymond said desperately. The words came out with a distortion that would have been unintelligible had Daniel not been anticipating them.

Daniel sipped from a mason jar that was sweating mightily in heat that was already nearing ninety degrees. Kentucky Bourbon and Coke had been the breakfast of Daniel's choosing, given that it was a holiday and all. The disheveled man shrugged. "What do you want me to do about it? Damn thing's nearly thirty years old."

Gaining his composure, Raymond said slowly, "Please help me fix the tractor."

"Raymond, it's a holiday. Take the day off. Have a drink with your old man," Daniel said, raising his jar. "It'll put hair on your chest, boy."

Raymond barred his teeth as he looked down at his father, half drunk and wearing a frayed bathrobe. "I don't have time."

"Suit yourself." Daniel ran the cold glass against his bare sternum.

Raymond turned abruptly and began to walk away. His father plucked an ice cube from the cooler at his feet and threw it at Raymond, hitting his son in the back. Raymond turned and looked over his shoulder. Daniel Gaines mouthed the words, *"Give up, Raymond."*

It was at this moment that Raymond found the thin line between love and hate to be no thicker than that betwixt pity and hate. Facing his father, Raymond could sense the conversion between one and the other taking place within him as surely as the cube of ice at his feet was turning to water.

Daniel returned the stare, waiting for Raymond to break down, capitulate, wilt, or even scream at him. Raymond did none of these things, but merely stood, his color returning to normal, his breathing slowing. It occurred to Daniel that he was no longer looking at a boy as he noted his son's threadbare jeans were a good two inches short.

Raymond sat on the bed of the truck surveying the scarred landscape consisting of knee-high stumps and deadened brush. He recalled reading about the battle of Gettysburg in his history class and how Lincoln had later paid tribute to the fallen, insisting that the sacrifice made must not be in vain. *Something good must come from this.* Drinking deeply from his water bottle, Raymond hopped off the flat bed of the truck and opened the rusting passenger door. Behind the seat he found a dented can of WD40, half a roll of duct tape, and a thick, stainless steel chain better than a dozen feet in length. With a calm clarity, Raymond looped the chain through the sleeves of his thick sweatshirt and wrapped the clothing in duct tape, creating a crude, padded yoke of sorts.

A single loop involving the stub that had once sported a branch was all Raymond needed to secure a log, and using his makeshift yolk, he began the long march up the slope, dragging the first of many lengths. Raymond started with logs of modest circumference and stopped to rest several times along the way. Seeing his unyielding son crest the hill log in tow, Daniel winced as he realized his hatred of Raymond was surpassed only by his hatred of self.

25

The sound of distant fireworks could be heard from inside the empty deli as Carlton loaded the industrial sized dishwasher. Trudy emerged from the kitchen with a freshly made submarine sandwich, which she began to wrap in clear plastic. Carlton glanced at Trudy as she finished wrapping the sandwich. He raised an eyebrow but said nothing until the girl put the substantial sandwich in her shoulder bag and untied her apron. "A little early to be packing up, don't you think?" Carlton tried his best to sound casual.

Trudy folded the apron and put it in her drawer. "I've cleared it with my uncle. Not that it's any of your business," she replied sharply, slinging the strap to the bag over her shoulder.

"Fair enough," Carlton said. He continued to load the dishwasher.

"And if you must know, I told him I'd come in early to do the floors tomorrow morning," Trudy said, heading for the door. She was just pushing the front door open when she heard Carlton question her once more.

"How would young Mercutio react if you were to show up sans sandwich?"

The question hung in the air thickly for a moment as Trudy absorbed the alliterative phrase. She tried to think of how Rochelle might have answered such a question. "He'd hunger for my body instead," Trudy said smugly. She was about to step into the night air when she stopped herself. "And don't you mean Romeo?"

Carlton had his back turned to her now, but Trudy could hear his tired voice say, "No. I mean Mercutio."

Trudy struggled for a moment, trying to recall Shakespeare's famous play from her tenth grade English class. Unable to make sense of Carlton's comment, Trudy shook her head and walked out the door in the direction of the fireworks and carnival music. The fireworks popping in the warm July night grew louder as Trudy approached the fairgrounds. She had been weighing Bobby's last words to her since he had uttered them. *I can't wait forever* really meant *I won't wait forever*, which translated into *I'll find someone who is ready if you aren't*. Of this Trudy was certain. And while she was not ready for the commitment and all that it entailed, she wasn't ready to be without Bobby, either. It had been so nice to have someone to talk to, someone to go places with, someone who was interested in her. In a way, it made up for Rochelle leaving, and Trudy had wished more than once that Rochelle could see her with Bobby.

Walking under the arches of the carnival entrance with the sandwich she had taken out of her shoulder bag, Trudy reasoned that there likely was not going to come a perfect time; that she would likely never be ready, and that it was better to take a chance on love rather than risk losing the first boy who had showed her any real interest since the fifth grade. Still, Trudy was not certain how she would react if Bobby pressed her to take that next step.

The night air smelled of buttery popcorn, candied apples, and cotton candy. The sound of the midway and piped-in music mingled with these smells as a multitude of bright lights from booths and fast moving rides surrounded Trudy on all sides. She had agreed to meet Bobby at nine o'clock by the Ferris wheel. Trudy looked up at the gigantic circular apparatus and pictured herself with Bobby. She imagined the wheel stuck for a few moments; nothing serious, just a chance for her and Bobby to enjoy the view while the world stood still for them. They would be holding hands, and he would look into her eyes and tell her he loved her. Then, as they were kissing, the music would resume and the wheel would begin to move again, as if inspired by the magic of their mutual love.

It was just before nine when she walked by a curtained photo booth, the kind that left patrons with a strip of keepsake black-and-white pictures after plugging in a half-dozen quarters. Trudy froze ten feet past the booth, cocking her head to one side as if listening for something faint and distant. Her face grew sullen. She walked back to the booth and tugged at the black curtain revealing a blond-haired girl giggling on top of Bobby Jasper's lap. One of Bobby's hands was up the girl's shirt, and he was kissing her lipstick-smeared mouth. Both stared at Trudy as if in momentary shock. Then, as if suddenly aware of the impropriety, Bobby quickly removed his hand from the bubbly blonde's shirt. This caused the girl to giggle once more until she slid from Bobby's lap as he pushed her aside and stood. An open forty-ounce bottle of beer in a brown paper bag toppled onto the grass at Trudy's feet when Bobby stood to face her.

Like most, Trudy had seen movies where a scorned woman slaps a lecherous cad, but her reaction was more of devastation than anger. It felt like she had been kicked in the chest, all the air from her lungs compressed without notice. Dropping the sandwich into the small pool of beery foam at her feet, Trudy put a hand to her mouth, which she realized was hanging open. Adding insult to injury, Trudy could read Bobby's simple mind as he thought for an instant about picking the sandwich up off the ground.

Just as Carlton had suggested, the sky *was* laced with brilliant fireworks, but Trudy could not see them through tears that brimmed from her eyes before running amok on her face as she ran back in the direction from which she had come. Trudy did not stop running until she approached the mobile home where she had lived since her father had left. Shouts and bitter screaming emanated from within the thinly insulated walls. A bottle could be heard breaking amid curses and shrieking. Trudy Thomas stood still in the night air, fireworks going off all around her. She began to sob deeply as it dawned on her that she had nowhere else to go.

26

Despite a level of exhaustion unlike any he had ever before encountered, Raymond lay in bed unable to sleep, listening to the faint pop of bottle rockets and various other fireworks in the distance. It was not the sound of the Independence Day celebration that kept him awake, though. Raymond was troubled by the clarity of three concepts solidifying in his mind, all of them pertaining to his father. The three had been mingling in the back of his mind for some time now. The first of these realizations involved the understanding that his father wanted Raymond to fail. At first, Raymond had felt that his father was simply lazy and unable to muster the energy necessary for the labor-intensive project that stood to enrich the man considerably. But Daniel's demeanor regarding the tractor's disrepair combined with his sudden penchant for fishing and his distinct mouthing of the words *give up*, left little doubt that the man was actively rooting against Raymond.

This revelation led Raymond to conclude that his father was embarrassed of him and didn't want Raymond to further shame him with ineptitude on the football field. Raymond knew that his father had attended North Carolina State on a football scholarship before injuring his knee and dropping out of the university his freshman year. It was something Raymond had learned from his mother and knew not to bring up with his father any more than the war that had so altered the man's disposition.

The two revelations hurt Raymond deeply, like a punch to the gut, only higher and in his chest. They also allowed Raymond to let go, once and for all, of the promise his mother had repeatedly made to Raymond before her death. Barbara Gaines had meant well, and may have even been correct, had she lived, but Raymond now knew that she had been wrong when she claimed that her husband would eventually reemerge as the loving father he once was. *That* Daniel Gaines, Raymond realized, had been forever lost somewhere thousands of miles from western Pennsylvania.

27

Through the window of her uncle's deli, Trudy watched Carlton do the work she was to have done in the morning. Except for a slumbering Roscoe, the man was alone, his spine bending as he slowly sloshed the mop back and forth across the floor. She could hear music faintly playing from the small transistor radio on the counter. It was old music, sung by singers Carlton had more than once sentimentally referred to as 'crooners'. Sometimes when he listened to these men with buttery voices while doing the dishes, a far-off look would come over Carlton's face, and Trudy would wonder what he was thinking.

Her heart was broken, and as she had been walking alone in the dark with no place to go, Trudy had been certain she could hurt no more than she currently did. Looking through the window at this old man, who had tried to warn her and was now doing her work, Trudy's heartache deepened, realizing how cruel she had been to Carlton at times. He had commented once, that everyone had a story, and for the first time Trudy wondered at Carlton's. So self-absorbed had she been, Trudy never really questioned what had brought this man to this place in time, and she felt ignorant and small for failing to do so.

Carlton looked up as Trudy entered the deli. One look at her face and the twin trails of eyeliner made Carlton wince knowingly. He set the mop in the bucket and embraced Trudy who came to him in silence. It was a long embrace, and one Trudy would never forget.

Together they made short work of what remained of Trudy's cleaning duties. Afterward the pair made their way outside and sat side by side at the table with their feet propped up on chairs and Roscoe between them. Both leaned back in their chairs so as to enjoy the fireworks that could still be seen over the rooftop of the building across the street. It was the first time they were truly at ease with one another, and Carlton handed Trudy a clean handkerchief knowing she would not take umbrage.

Trudy dipped the handkerchief in her glass of water on the table and began to wipe the mascara from her face. "Mercutio was the fickle one," she said, handing the cloth back to Carlton.

"Right," Carlton nodded. He stifled a chuckle as he looked at the smeared handkerchief for a moment before tossing it on the table.

The heartbroken girl half expected him to say something along the lines of *I told you so*. Trudy knew that she had it coming and told herself she deserved a measure of admonishment. Instead, Carlton remained silent, only extending his pack of cigarettes, one pulled out halfway.

"Thanks," Trudy said, removing the cigarette. She leaned toward the man and allowed him to light her cigarette before lighting his own. Both exhaled simultaneously, and it was silent except for the distant pop of a bottle rocket.

"Quite the firework display," Carlton said, admiring a particularly colorful shower of lights.

"You should have seen it last year," Trudy commented.

"Well a bicentennial celebration *should* be exceptional. Not every country makes it to two hundred years, you know," Carlton said.

"I suppose," Trudy said. "I'm not really the patriotic type." Trudy hoped Carlton would not ask her to explain. Already emotionally racked, she did not want to discuss losing her brother in a war she regarded as meaningless. "Who is W. S.?" Trudy asked quickly, referring to the initials on Carlton's silver lighter.

Carlton plucked the lighter from the table and deposited it in his shirt pocket. "No one important."

"Don't tell me you stole it," Trudy teased.

"No," Carlton chuckled. "Not really."

"A woman, perhaps?" Trudy raised an eyebrow suggestively the way Carlton had done with her on occasion.

Carlton shook his head. "Just someone from a previous life," he said.

"Okay," Trudy said. "I can take a hint."

"Since when?" Carlton smiled, and Trudy wondered if he was alluding to her love life. As if curious himself, Roscoe lifted his head from his paws and looked at Trudy.

"I notice he's not limping anymore," Trudy said, gesturing toward the mutt.

"He finally let me take a look at his paw the other day," Carlton said. "There was a pretty nasty thorn in there."

"Sounds Biblical," Trudy commented, racking her brain for where she knew of such a story.

Carlton chuckled. "Aesop, actually," he replied. "If you're thinking of Androcles, that is."

Trudy snapped her fingers. "Right. He was the slave that befriended the lion by taking the thorn out of his paw. Then, when he got thrown in the cage with the lion it wouldn't eat him because the lion remembered how Androcles had helped him."

Carlton smiled. "I think you retain a lot more from your literary studies than you want to let on."

"So how do *you* know so much about literature?" Trudy asked, determined to change the focus away from her studies.

"Used to teach it," Carlton replied quietly.

"In high school?" Trudy sounded surprised.

"College." Carlton took another drag on his cigarette.

"Wow. I had no idea," Trudy said, still in shock.

"It was a long time ago," Carlton replied simply.

"Previous lifetime?" she prompted, using Carlton's own words.

"You could say that," Carlton replied.

Both were quiet for a moment as if lost in thought. "I don't get it," Trudy said, baffled. "What are you doing here? Doing this?" She pointed to the deli behind them.

Carlton sighed deeply, and his brow furrowed. "I got fired," he said, his voice full of resignation.

Trudy gave him a woeful look, asking with a measure of trepidation, "An affair with a student?"

Carlton laughed. "No."

It was the first time Trudy could remember seeing her friend really laugh, and she laughed too, almost in relief. When they had both stopped it was quiet for a moment. For reasons she could not explain, Trudy sensed she had stumbled onto Carlton's story. She also sensed it would change how she viewed him forever. "It's okay. You don't have to tell me," she said.

"It's alright. Part of the penance," Carlton said, toying with the lighter he had unknowingly removed from his pocket again. He pointed to the glass of beer on the table, and for a moment he had something that resembled the faraway look on his face that Trudy had observed more than once. "Too many of those," he said, still pointing at the beer glass.

Carlton stared sadly into the darkness, lost in his own thoughts. Trudy hesitated at seeing his sadness and then offered Carlton his own handkerchief in a halfhearted attempt at levity. It worked, because he looked at the black makeup on the square and grimaced theatrically.

They both laughed again until Carlton looked at Trudy and said, "One can't be certain, but I suspect you'd be a very pretty girl without all the warpaint."

Trudy laughed again. "I know I'd have more time in the morning," she said, wiping a strand of hair from her eyes.

Carlton looked at Trudy's black boots but left them alone. "And while you're at it, you might lose some of that hardware," he continued, touching his earlobe and hoping he wasn't pressing his luck.

Trudy instinctively touched her own ear, where a half-dozen pieces of metal were lodged. "I'd certainly be lighter," she shrugged.

28

Following the Fourth of July revelations regarding his father, Raymond began a daily pattern that no longer involved the meticulous breakdown of a calendar in relation to acres cleared or units of lumber to be brought topside. Raymond Gaines, in nearly robotic fashion, became the sole engine of a cycle that involved straining nearly every muscle in his body in defiance of gravity, while allowing for rest as he returned down the slope, burdened only by the dusty, chain-link tail that trailed faithfully after him. At the bottom, Raymond would drink deeply from the store of milk jugs kept in the shade of the truck, allowing some to cascade over his red locks, before securing the next log.

The tandem of soreness and sunburn served to antagonize his every nerve during waking moments, but when Raymond put his head on his pillow at night he entered another realm and awoke with renewed determination. He found it strange that he could not remember a single dream. It was as though every fiber of his mental and physical being were directed toward the task at hand.

Thoughts of quitting or even slowing were vanquished any time Raymond would see his father sprawled in the lawn chair staring ahead at God only knew what. The man would no longer meet Raymond's stares, focusing instead on targeting nearby bugs with an occasional volley of tobacco-laced sputum.

Days turned into weeks turned into August. Raymond remained undeterred, despite the undeniable factors involving too much lumber and too little time. It was no longer about football or even his father. To Raymond, the project became about the force of sheer will. It mattered not that the logs were now larger and stops for rest were all but eliminated. No plan or scheme had been hatched, only that the land would be cleared, or Raymond would die trying.

29

Bobby Jasper stood outside Joe's Deli nervously sucking on what remained of a cigarette stub. He tossed the butt on the sidewalk, stepped on it, and exhaled deeply before jamming his hands in his jean pockets and walking in the door that Mr. Renton held open for him. Bobby had been waiting for the Rentons to leave so that he could talk to Trudy alone. He hoped the nosey old man, who served as the cook, would be back in the kitchen somewhere.

Bobby took a deep breath and approached Trudy who was behind both the counter and the cover of *Tale of Two Cities*, in which she appeared to be deeply engrossed. Pulling his hands from his pockets, Bobby placed them on the counter and cleared his throat so as to get Trudy's attention. When this failed Bobby cleared his throat again and said, "Trudy, can I talk to you for a minute?"

Trudy lowered the book. Bobby's eyes registered shock as he studied Trudy's face, which was radiant and natural, absent the heavy makeup and metal that had been the norm when they dated. He also noticed for the first time that her hair was now a natural, auburn brown color. Trudy smiled demurely, no sign of animosity on her countenance. "Would you like a menu?" she said sweetly.

Bobby stepped back involuntarily. "Ah, no. I, I came here. I didn't come here to eat. I…" he stammered.

Trudy's smile remained, but her sparkling eyes darkened like heavy rainclouds. "Then perhaps you'd better leave," she said.

Bobby backed up, still taking in the change that had come over his former girlfriend. She maintained her smile until Bobby turned and walked out the door. Trudy turned over her shoulder and smiled at Carlton before lowering her eyes to the book once more. Carlton, who had a smirk of his own playing about his mouth, asked, "How's the book coming?"

Trudy's smirk resembled that of her friend's as she replied, "People are losing their heads."

"The French," Carlton mused, then stopped short of completing his thought.

"You ever been to France?" Trudy asked.

Carlton turned to the grill. "Once."

"What was it like?"

"Beauty plagued by misery," Carlton replied over his shoulder.

The phrase reminded her briefly of Rochelle. "Sounds like an interesting trip," Trudy commented.

"You could say that," Carlton murmured.

30

Friday, August 16

Daniel Gaines had not provided the conflict or resistance Jack Parson had anticipated. The man wouldn't even meet his eyes. He just sat in the shaded portion of the front porch, staring ahead, only pointing in the direction that Raymond might be found. Sweat beaded Daniel's forehead, and Parson was briefly reminded of a hike through the jungle in which his canteen had long been empty. A firefight had broken the silence after his unit stumbled on a small pocket of resistance. Parson had forgotten his thirst as survival leapfrogged past thirst in a hierarchy of importance. When the three-minute battle had ended Jack's unit had come upon the small group of Viet Cong that had been killed. Several of the parched men alongside Jack had reached for the canteens that were strewn among the dead. Each of the men coughed, sputtered, and spit out the salt water they had greedily gulped. Parson looked to the dead, all of whom still had their eyes open, more than one with a smile playing on cooling, gray lips.

Parson listened for the sound of a Cat or truck and heard only a faint but high-pitched whine as might be made by a small electric drill operating at high revolutions per minute. The noise grew louder as he walked toward a massive collection of stacked logs stretching yard after yard better than waist-high. The coach reasoned that Raymond would be resting or fixing the power tool that could be heard, the heat of the day being incompatible with heavy work.

Parson was soon proven wrong as he passed the last of the stacked logs and came upon the sight of Raymond pulling a log easily twice his weight with an ease that strained credulity. The coach's jaw dropped as he quickly realized this was not the same Raymond Gaines he had known some two months earlier. His former student no longer resembled the gangly boy in PE class. Coming toward him with fierce determination etched in his face, was a man, the likes of which would have sent Michelangelo in search of stone. Easily twenty-five to thirty pounds of muscle had been evenly distributed on Raymond's frame, which was now just shy of six and-a-half feet in height. The boy's fair skin had been overwhelmed by freckles, until no longer fair, but brown. Samson came to mind, as the red mop had become a cascade of untamed fire over the course of the summer.

Quadriceps like banded steel propelled long, determined uphill strides. Calf muscles bulged above boots that sought purchase amid dust and rock. A purple intersection forming the letter X crossed a massive bare chest that was deeply bruised from alternating the cruel Spartan yoke. The physical specimen, unlike any high schooler Parson had ever seen, had been focusing on the rutted ground just feet in front of him. Sensing a presence, Raymond looked upslope, slow to show recognition of his teacher and coach. The high-pitched whine that had emanated from deep within the teen suddenly stopped.

Parson had seen this look of slow or begrudging recognition before. His unit had once freed three P.O.W.s after securing a village outside of Chu Lai. The three men had looked upon their liberators with distrust for several moments before elation and civilizing effects gradually dawned in their eyes.

The look of fierceness - or even hatred - faded, and Raymond stopped and straightened his broad back. He tried to say something but was betrayed by vocal cords that hadn't been exercised in better than a month.

At the bottom of the slope ten minutes later, Parson stood in Raymond's considerable shadow as the youth drained the remaining quarter of a water jug. The young man's pants had been cut off above the knee and were split to mid-thigh by quads that could no longer be contained by the frayed denim. Calloused hands no longer had use of gloves that had long since been shredded anyway. Looking at Raymond standing against the sun, Parson was reminded of the process involved in the creation of tempered steel.

At the top of the slope Raymond released the especially large and cumbersome log Parson had awkwardly helped him drag. The two men shook hands and Raymond descended like Sisyphus, to repeat his task yet again. Parson watched as Raymond made his way down the slope, a look of bewildered awe playing on the coach's face. Minutes later Parson walked by the trailer toward his truck and was halted abruptly by the sound of the elder Gaines' voice cracking much the way Raymond's had. "My boy's all yours, soon as the slope's cleared, Coach. Should be ready 'bout the time playoffs roll around." Gaines laughed cruelly until he began to cough and rasp.

Parson looked at the long column of logs on the ridge and noted the pattern that had them gaining in circumference. The pattern was consistent with the strength and mass that Raymond had attained as the summer had progressed, his gradually increasing strength allowing him to bring topside bigger and bigger logs. Ironically, Parson noted, looking at man in the bathrobe, Raymond's strength coincided with the notable withering of his father.

Parson had been determined to get away without an interchange with the pathetic man. He turned and faced Raymond's father, waiting until the man's coughing subsided, and said with more compassion than bitterness, "If having a son like Raymond can't bring you back, I guess nothing could. I'm sorry for your loss, soldier."

At the end of the dirt driveway, Parson stopped and put his forehead against the steering wheel, not knowing whether to call Children's Protective Services or a Florida State scout with whom he had served. He watched in the rearview mirror as Raymond's father met him at the top of the slope. The man lobbed an empty beer bottle at his son, who raised his arms in defense, much as Raymond had against the first football Tommy had thrown his way the previous spring.

31

When Carlton came out to the tables in front of the deli he found Trudy and Roscoe waiting for him. The dog wagged his tail, while the teenage girl could scarcely contain the smile that she'd kept under wraps while working alongside her elderly companion all afternoon and evening. Carlton looked at her with amusement, saying only, "What gives?" as he sat wearily in the chair across the table from her. Trudy pushed his half of the tips to the center of the table. "You've got more than tips on your mind, Trudy," Carlton grinned.

Trudy could no longer contain herself. She pulled a folded sheaf of paper from her bag and proudly handed it to Carlton. The man unfolded it before studying the paper for a moment. A wide smile broke on his face as the *A+* in red ink at the top of the first page registered in his mind. He began reading the paper aloud. "No greater theme can exist in the world of literature than Dickens' depiction of a man loving a woman so much that he'd give his own life to ensure her happiness." Carlton's eyes began to water, forcing him to stop.

Tears had also formed in the wells of Trudy's eyes as Carlton continued. After reading the entire contents aloud, his eyes broke from the paper. "I'm proud of you, Trudy. You have all the makings of a lady. You can literally write your own ticket in this world!" he exclaimed.

Trudy laughed, embarrassed by what she perceived as Carlton's overreaction. "It's just a paper," she said, casting her eyes toward the sidewalk at her feet.

"A paper representing the best of you and your potential," Carlton gushed as he continued to pour over the paper in his hand.

A pall came over Trudy. She suddenly felt silly for having shown Carlton the essay. For a moment it had felt good, the strange and unfamiliar warmth that accompanied having someone actually proud of her. But it faded quickly as certain socioeconomic realities crowded to the forefront of Trudy's thinking. It showed on her countenance, and Carlton asked her what was the matter.

"You'll have to forgive me," she said bitterly, "if the paper feels a little light when weighed against a broken home, poverty, a failed junior year, and a mom who changes boyfriends more often than underwear."

Carlton was not to be deterred and leaned forward holding the paper toward Trudy as if it were a lifeline of sorts. "All the more reason to hitch your wagon to this star. Use the pain and frustration in your life to fuel your gift. Trudy, you can write!" Carlton continued, shaking the paper with emphasis.

She took the paper and looked at the large red $A+$ accompanied by several superlatives from her teacher. A tear from her cheek dropped onto the crimson letter, and Trudy instinctively rubbed it away, smearing the mark.

32

Monday, August 19, the first day of daily doubles, saw no discontinuation or even diminishment of Raymond's Herculean efforts until just before noon when the weary teen suddenly stopped. He lifted the yoke over his head and let it drop to the packed soil at his feet. It landed with a musical conclusion that was lost on Raymond. The vast, wide-open, stubbled space around him made Raymond feel suddenly exposed, and yet all alone at the same time. He gazed at the shorn slope that rose in front of him before sweeping his eyes over the multitude of stumps for which he was responsible. Where once there had been beauty, tranquility, and an abundance of wildlife, there now existed nothing but a sort of barren wasteland. It was conceivable, Raymond had once thought, that this clear-cutting, could be justified if something good came of it. But nothing good had, only a cementing of the divide Raymond felt between himself and his father. Raymond looked at the hundreds of remaining logs strewn haphazardly about the raped landscape. A feeling of futility washed over the young man, and he raised his weary arms toward the sky above as if pleading for an explanation.

One couldn't distinguish if it was sweat, tears, or both that poured from Raymond's face only moments later, as he watched an old, yellow school bus pull up close to the wave of logs at the top of the slope. Coach Parson, wearing overalls, a t-shirt, baseball cap, and gloves, exited the bus followed by nearly fifty of Raymond's similarly clad teammates. They were armed with chains, ropes, and water jugs. Daniel Gaines stared in amazement as the entire football team exited the bus. Finally able to drink in what was happening, Raymond's father went into the trailer and locked the door.

The team stood at the top of the slope and surveyed the task at hand. Raymond wiped moisture from his face and stared in awe at the group above him. Seeing the physical transformation that had overtaken Raymond, they returned the stare with no less awe. Coach Robinson, who was last off the bus, broke through the line of players, took one look at Raymond, and muttered under his breath, "Hot damn tipping point."

33

The diner was nearly empty with only a young couple sharing a booth, each staring into the eyes of the other as they drank a milkshake, the two straws linking them in a strange show of symmetry. Trudy was drying the dishes as Carlton washed them.

"Do you miss literature?" she suddenly asked. She had tried to make the question sound as though it had just occurred to her, but both knew this was not the case, just as they both understood that Trudy meant *teaching* literature, but had been unable to phrase the question as such.

"I don't do without," Carlton hedged, handing her a heavy skillet to dry.

"I mean teaching," she said, her resolve firming.

"Sure. But I still read," Carlton said.

"For the escape?" Trudy asked, aware that she had just provided her own reason for enjoying the pursuit.

"For the immersion," Carlton responded.

Trudy thought for a moment before asking, "What do you mean?"

Carlton stopped washing the dishes, leaned on the sink so as to take pressure off his aching back, and said in a wistful voice, "With the possible exception of art, literature is the one realm in which one can bathe in the wash of sheer genius from great minds throughout the centuries."

Trudy stared at him as she weighed words that she wished Rochelle could have heard. After absorbing them and locking the words in a mental file she kept, Trudy said earnestly, "Maybe I'm not the only one who should be writing."

Carlton offered no response, instead growing quiet and somber as he resumed rinsing the dishes in the sink. Trudy did not know what to make of the change that had come over her friend in the blink of an eye. She wondered if she had said something wrong and decided to press the matter by asking, "Have you ever tried?"

"Sure," Carlton said.

"You get published?" Trudy prompted, her curiosity piqued.

"Once," was all she got by way of response as Carlton unplugged the sink and rinsed his hands before drying them off with the dingy towel that always seemed to be slung over his shoulder.

34

Mornings of the first week of daily doubles were spent on a new and unconventional form of conditioning at Coach Parson's behest and direction. One look at Raymond convinced his teammates that logging unencumbered by technology was the way to achieve incredible fitness and possibly even the notice of girls. Two and sometimes three of Raymond's teammates struggled with logs the size Raymond hauled with regularity. The pairs strained with determination as Raymond pulled even on the trail, often winking as he left them behind. The team sang as they worked, and Raymond, who couldn't hear a note, was nonetheless convinced he was in the midst of a chorus of angels. Afternoons were spent back on the field incorporating plays, practicing special teams, and scrimmaging, while Raymond remained on the slope, toiling by himself until dark.

By the end of the afternoon practice on Friday, Coach Parson felt very positive about how his team had rallied around a cause. He could sense their cohesion, camaraderie, and good will. In addition, there existed an inexplicable sense of empathy as well as an element of teamwork that Parson had never seen on a football field before as either a player or a coach. After gathering the team on one knee before him, Parson told the attentive group to rest and relax their bruises and muscle strains over the weekend because the following week would bring on full-contact drills and scrimmaging. When the players had taken the equipment to the shed and headed to the locker room, Parson turned to his old friend, Coach Robinson. Simultaneously they both said, "This year's going to be special." It seemed almost eerie coming out of both mouths at once, but there also seemed an undeniable element of destiny in play.

Neglecting his own yard work, Jack Parson arrived early Saturday morning to help Raymond once again. Never had a coach been so pleased at the willful insubordination of his squad, as Parson was that same morning, when, to a man, the team showed up, piled in cars and pickup trucks, to help Raymond finish the job.

Hours later, Daniel Gaines walked out of the trailer so dehydrated he couldn't muster the saliva to spit. He stood at the loading zone, staring in disbelief as log after log made its way up the incline. An hour before the job was completed, Gaines got in his lime green pickup truck and left without saying a word. When his sore and weary teammates had all left, Raymond found himself standing beside his head coach, both experiencing a level of bliss neither would soon forget. Parson took a folded paper out of his pocket, handed it to the exhausted young man, clapped him gently on the back, and told him to be ready to play come Monday.

After watching the dust settle as his coach's truck drove out of sight, Raymond unfolded the schedule of games that would put his name on the lips of many a college football scout.

35

Trudy was sitting impatiently in the bright sun outside the deli at the table she and Carlton frequented after work. She crushed her cigarette and got up when she saw Carlton shuffle around the corner with a bag of groceries in his arms. Trudy approached the weary man who greeted her with, "Good afternoon, Trudy. Everything alright?" He appeared somewhat alarmed that his young friend could not wait for him to get to the deli where they were both scheduled to work the afternoon and evening shifts.

No return salutation was forthcoming from the girl. Instead, Trudy broke in with, "I looked in the library. I even had the librarian look you up. She couldn't find you either. I want to read what you wrote."

Carlton smiled with a pained expression marking his eyes. Trudy had the look of a youth who needed someone to believe in, thought they had found such a person, and now feared the rug being pulled out from under them. Carlton continued walking, saying over his shoulder, "For good reason."

Trudy stood in disbelief where she had initially accosted Carlton. "You mean you lied to me?"

Carlton continued into the diner where he refrigerated several items from his grocery bag. Trudy followed him into the building, staring at Carlton with an incredulous look on her face while he donned his apron behind the counter.

In the same tone she had expressed her disdain at learning Rochelle Martz had left her on her own for the summer, Trudy screamed, "You fill me full of hot air about writing and then lie about it? Hitch a wagon to a star? Are you kidding me? I believed you!"

The guilt etched in Carlton's face was palpable. He hung his head and walked into the kitchen, leaving Trudy standing in front of the counter determined not to spill the tears that threatened to crest over her eyes.

The two worked in silence for much of the afternoon and evening, talking only when serving their customers necessitated words between them. Having worked together so well and for so many hours, very little needed to be said, but the tension was thick as Trudy scrubbed the tabletops, and Carlton mopped the floor in silence at the end of the evening. Trudy continued scrubbing as Carlton slipped away for a few moments. He went up to his apartment above the deli and came back with an item, which he proceeded to slip into Trudy's backpack when her back was turned.

Both knew there would be no *table talk,* as they had dubbed their end of the day cigarette sharing ritual. After leaving Carlton's share of the tips on a counter, Trudy came out of the kitchen, grabbed her backpack, and headed for the door.

"Good night," Carlton offered timidly.

Trudy did not so much as look at the man as she responded curtly while walking out the door, "Good night."

Fifteen minutes later, Trudy had made her way past her mother and Dirk who were watching a game show in the dark. As if drained of energy, Trudy shut the door to her room and sat on the bed with her face in her hands. She was amazed at how one lie from an old man that she hadn't even known five months earlier could have such a deflating effect on her. She thought back on the conversations they had shared. Carlton seemed to know so much about literature, but now Trudy doubted he had even been a professor. For all she knew, the man could be a homeless vagrant who had merely read a few books and wandered from town to town.

Still, Trudy admitted to herself, she had changed for the better as a result of her association with this enigmatic man. She could feel it in every aspect of her life; from the approach she had taken with summer school, to dealing with unsavory characters like Dirk and Bobby Jasper. Trudy looked at the small mirror above her dresser where she had taped her first *A+* paper. As a bonus, Trudy now enjoyed reading literature and loved to write, feeling confident in her ability to create her own steadily improving fiction, which was increasingly well received by her teachers. None of this, Trudy had to acknowledge, would likely have come about without Carlton. Even if the man was not what he had purported to be, Trudy decided, she was all the better for having known him.

With this in mind, Trudy got up and changed into her nightclothes. Determined to write a few lines in her spiral, she dumped the contents of her backpack on the bedspread. Among them was a thick and weathered paperback book that Trudy did not recognize. She picked it up and held the book under the reading light by her bed. The author's name was William Stroud, but on the back cover was an unmistakable picture of a much younger and happier Carlton Smith.

36

Raymond awoke the morning of his first day of school to the sound of trucks pulling into the loading zone. The eighteen wheel flatbeds would take the last of the Hemlock and leave Raymond's father with the proceeds of Raymond's labor in conjunction with his grandfather's forethought. None of this mattered to Raymond though, who greeted the day knowing only that his dream of being able to play high school football was finally on the cusp of being realized.

*   *   *   *   *   *

The dawning of that same day saw Trudy Thomas finishing William Stroud's award-winning novel, the edge of the cresting sun greeting Trudy as she looked out the window just moments after closing the book. Trudy stretched for a moment before putting on her coat and slipping out of the house, careful not to awaken her mother or Dirk.

37

Foam and cold, salty water washed up over Carlton's legs and torso until it engulfed his face, causing him to sputter. By the third time it happened, he had learned to hold his breath until the wave retreated, leaving him to once again contemplate getting to his feet. It was more easily thought than done, as tremendous pressure bore down on his back. It seemed the water was taking longer and longer to retreat, and Carlton knew that if he did not get up soon he would drown. Always before it was when his lungs seemed about to burst that Carlton would awaken with a gasp, aware that he was drenched not by the surf but by his own sweat.

This time it was Roscoe's barking that awoke Carlton, the sound of frantic pounding on the door having awakened the animal sleeping at the foot of the old man's bed. Within moments Carlton answered the door while wiping his damp brow with the sleeve of his terry cloth robe. He was unshaven and looked disheveled and even a little confused as he slipped a pair of glasses on his face in an effort to recognize who had been pounding on his door at six a.m.

"Who the hell?" he squawked, his voice catching on something in his throat.

"I am the hell Trudy," the teen said with enthusiasm as she sprang into the room.

"What's the matter?" Carlton asked with alarm.

"Why did you quit?" Trudy responded. "You're wonderful! Why did you stop writing?" she demanded. Her tone changed for a moment as she studied the old man. "Why are you sweating?"

"You rescued me from a bad dream," Carlton muttered before removing the glasses from his face and wiping his eyes with the palm of his hand.

Trudy stood on the balls of her feet and clasped her hands together. "Why did you quit?" she asked for the second time.

"Calm down, girl. Just calm down," Carlton said, trudging toward the small kitchen as he secured the rope on his robe.

Trudy's enthusiasm remained unbridled. "I don't understand. You're so gifted! Please tell me why you didn't write more," she begged.

"How do you know I didn't?" the old man inquired as he began to fill a coffee pot with water from the tap.

"You told me you were just published the one time," Trudy said impatiently.

Carlton nodded. "That's right. I guess I did," he said. Carlton measured some coffee grounds, poured some water, and turned on the machine before sitting at the small kitchen table. "Sit down, Trudy. Just sit a moment while I get my bearings."

Trudy complied. She leaned close and beamed a smile on Carlton as he continued to rub his eyes. "I'm waiting," she said with obvious anticipation.

Carlton shook off the final remnants of the dream from which he had been awakened. "I only gave you that book so you would know I was genuine in my appraisal of your talents,"

Carlton said, putting his glasses back on. The coffee began to percolate noisily in the background as the rich smell wafted their way.

"I believe you. And I'm sorry I ever doubted you. I just don't understand why you quit. Why you are holed up here in this worthless town like some kind of refugee," Trudy blurted.

Carlton chuckled. "Refugee," he repeated with a chuckle. "That's good, Trudy."

"What happened to you?" Trudy implored.

After biting his lower lip and gathering his thoughts, Carlton began, "You remember why I said I lost my teaching position?"

"You said you drank too much," Trudy said, her enthusiasm dampening slightly as she recalled the faraway look on Carlton's face as he had revealed the fact.

"Yes," Carlton conceded. "But that was only part of the story."

"I'm listening," Trudy said quietly, knowing that for better or worse, she was about to finally learn Carlton's story.

Carlton rose and went to the refrigerator where he withdrew a small carton of creamer, which he smelled after opening. He then took two mugs from a cabinet and poured coffee in each. "Cream and sugar?" he asked, looking at Trudy.

"Please," Trudy nodded.

After pouring sugar and cream into the coffee, Carlton put a spoon in each and carefully handed Trudy her mug. Carlton sat down heavily at the table and began in earnest after closing his eyes for a moment.

"I had a beautiful, loving wife and daughter, tenure at a prestigious university, and the privilege of seeing my name grace the New York Times Best Sellers list with my debut novel. Some might say I had the world by the tail, Trudy," Carlton said with reserve.

"You drank it all away?" Trudy asked.

"If only it were so," Carlton returned, stirring the contents of his own mug.

"I don't understand," Trudy said, her eyes riveted on Carlton.

"Rather," Carlton continued, "returning from a Christmas faculty party late one evening, I killed a family of five while under the influence of a good deal of scotch." Trudy's eyes dropped from Carlton's to the table. Carlton winced himself. "The university, rightfully, dismissed me soon thereafter. I lost every penny I owned to the surviving family. Rightfully as well, I might add."

"And your wife?" Trudy could not help herself from asking.

Carlton sighed. "My wife soon grew weary of my pity and self-loathing. I can't blame her for leaving. I probably would have lost respect for her if she hadn't," Carlton added.

"Your daughter?" Trudy asked, not really wanting to know.

"My wife remarried, a well-to-do businessman who ended up adopting my daughter, who had all but disowned me by that time. I can't say I blame her, either," Carlton concluded.

Trudy and Carlton drank their coffee in silence as Trudy absorbed the story she had just heard. It sickened her that Carlton could be responsible for the deaths of innocent people, but at the same time her heart ached for what it had clearly done to a man she still regarded as decent.

Her head still swimming, Trudy heard herself say, "You told me to draw on my pain as a writer."

"I did," Carlton conceded, before taking a drink from the mug.

"It sounds like you have a full tank." Trudy tried to force a smile.

Again, Carlton nodded. "Quite the reservoir, my dear."

And then, as if it just occurred to her, Trudy said, "You loved to write, didn't you?"

"I did."

"So?" Trudy pressed.

Carlton finished his coffee before responding, "So it is a small penance, but one I feel I must observe."

"You don't think you've paid enough?" Trudy asked, thinking of all Carlton had forfeited.

"I don't believe it's possible," Carlton insisted.

"You still read," Trudy prompted.

"Call me Tantalus," Carlton said with a bittersweet smile.

"Water up to your chin but condemned to eternal thirst?" Trudy said, attempting to recall Greek mythology from two years earlier.

"Bright girl," Carlton remarked, a smile on his lips but great sadness in his eyes.

38

His first week of football practice revealed nothing special about the first year player. Looking every bit as inexperienced as he was, Raymond had trouble picking up instruction and often resorted to following the cues of other players. Even when he did understand, Raymond often had to think rather than react, since none of what he was doing was second nature to the gridiron novice. This was only half of what made him appear slow and unwieldy. Having expended everything he had both physically and mentally in a preternatural effort, Raymond came crashing down, as his body demanded healing and rest. Parson recognized this from spending a week in bed on furlough once, using every minute to restore his spent energy. With this in mind, the head coach still held out hope for his project player, offering him encouragement and praise whenever an opportunity arose.

Tommy Wilkins took Raymond out for burgers and Cokes, spending time explaining fundamentals, techniques, and strategies in a setting that relaxed Raymond and allowed him to ask questions. This was invaluable to Raymond, since despite being an offensive player, Tommy understood all the defensive schemes, because he was constantly forced to read them. No one had ever invited Raymond to their home before the senior quarterback told Raymond the guys were all meeting at Tommy's after the last of the daily double practices.

Three picnic tables were lined up on the front lawn, and some of the fellows were already seated without shirts when

Raymond laid his squeaky, old ten-speed on the lawn. Tommy's girlfriend and a few of her friends, including a girl named Karen Stevens, had electric razors and extension cords in place. Raymond made it a point to wait in Karen's line. Soon the tabletops were covered with shorn locks of all different shades and lengths. Raymond's flaming tresses joined his teammates, and they all laughed and jeered one another as they posed for a less than formal team photo, while imagining a breeze that cooled their newly shorn scalps. Best of all, Karen took Raymond over to his bike and smiled at him while she put some of the oil she had used on the shears onto Raymond's bone-dry bike chain.

That night Raymond put on his uniform as soon as his father left to play pool at a tavern in town. The players had been urged to take the uniforms home so that parents could take pictures before the uniforms became stained and the helmet paint chipped. Raymond had no such allusions about his father wanting to take a senior picture of his son in uniform, but he had taken the gear home anyway. First, Raymond put on the golden pad-filled pants. Then he fumbled with the straps that went under his arms before lacing the breastplate on the shoulder pads that made it so he had to turn sideway to get through doorways. It took several minutes to slide the white mesh jersey with golden letters and the number forty-seven over his shoulder pads since Raymond had no teammate available to help him. Finally, Raymond donned the golden helmet, which had been touched up with a special spray paint after practice earlier that same day.

Standing in front of the cracked mirror in the bathroom, Raymond sneered and got in a defensive position as if poised to make a tackle. In his mind he ran over some of the defensive stunts Coach Robinson had employed as well as the techniques he had learned to avoid and get past blockers. *Pay attention to the snap-count tendencies by reading the quarterback's lips. Watch the quarterback's eyes as well,* Raymond reminded himself. *Hope the QB telegraphs where he wants to throw the ball. Look at the direction the offensive linemen point their toes. Pay attention to the snap-count tendencies by watching the quarterback's mouth.*

The door to the trailer swung open and Daniel lurched into the dwelling. Raymond straightened and stared in surprise at his father who looked at Raymond and muttered a curse. Daniel was on the verge of saying something about Raymond's uniform never needing to be washed, but stopped short. At nearly six and-a-half feet in height and two hundred and thirty pounds, Raymond was more physically imposing than most of the players Daniel had known at North Carolina State. He realized any high school coach would be crazy not to see what Raymond could do on the field. Instead, Daniel renewed his sneer and simply said, "At least they didn't give you *my* number," before grabbing a pack of cigarettes by the sink and leaving again with an air of disgust.

39

Trudy reread Carlton's novel hoping it would help her make sense of the tragic story he had imparted. The portrayal of love that had emerged from a war-torn Europe was in stark contrast to the lives that had been ended by the author's decision to get behind the wheel after an evening of imbibing. Try as she might, Trudy could not fathom the same man being responsible for both any more than she could reconcile in her mind the loss of her brother in a war that was equally senseless.

Many nights Trudy had lain awake imagining a meeting with the Viet Cong soldier that had killed Jimmy. For years she had thought about what she would like to say and do to the man, whose face she could never quite conjure. The hatred she had for this man, who had cut her brother's life short, frightened Trudy. Yet, she often intentionally summoned scenarios so that she could mete out some form of justice, even if only in her own mind. After the second reading of Carlton's novel – she somehow could not bring herself to think of him as William Stroud – Trudy had realized that somewhere out in the cold world beyond her home, someone was likely thinking of her friend and mentor in much the same way that she thought of the faceless soldier who had pulled the pin of a grenade before lobbing it in the direction of Private First Class James Thomas.

40

The physical inactivity involved with sitting in class for better than six hours a day has always made some students fidgety and anxious. For Raymond though, it was better than bed rest. While every fiber in his body took the opportunity to knit, renew, and regenerate, his mind was stimulated both socially and academically. His buzzed haircut marked membership to a club that meant purpose, pride, and inclusion. Practice after school was nothing compared to doubles or the rigors he had put himself through on the North Slope, and things soon began to click on the field as Raymond rapidly recovered.

As he began to heal and recharge, Raymond proved the speed he had demonstrated the previous spring had been no fluke. Indeed, it had been improved upon. If there was a concern it was Raymond's reluctance to be physical. While he could take a hit and come up grinning, Raymond seemed reticent when it came time to initiate physical contact with the other players. This contrasted greatly with the collisions Raymond initiated with the tackling sled, often driving the six hundred pound apparatus in a way that Coach Robinson had never seen. Since the team was deep on the offensive line and Raymond had already proven to have hands of stone, moving him to offense made little sense. Coaches Parson and Robinson agreed that given Raymond's size, speed, and relative inexperience he would be best utilized at defensive end, if only they could get him to be aggressive when tackling ball carriers made of flesh and bones.

41

Fall was in the air, and Trudy wore a sweater and Carlton a windbreaker as they sat in front of the deli dividing the day's tips and enjoying their end of the day cigarette. No mention had been made of the story Carlton had revealed to Trudy, yet it hung in the autumn air as surely as the blue-grey smoke that circled in the light above them. For days Trudy had tried to make sense of the tragedy that had befallen her gentle friend. For some reason, she could not entirely explain, even to herself, she wanted to make things right; bring healing to Carlton in the way that she recognized he had done for her as well as Roscoe, who sat in his customary spot between them.

It may have been this yearning that prompted her to ask, "So, who are some of your favorite writers?"

Carlton leaned back in his chair and gazed at the heavens through the cloud of their making. It was clear to Trudy that she had at least succeeded in temporarily taking him to a good place as the former professor searched his brain for the answer to her question. "Oh, I don't know," he mused. "So many from which to choose."

Trudy marveled at the way he spoke. Not ending sentences with prepositions somehow earned Carlton a spot in Trudy's mind alongside some of the old film stars who beseeched and bequeathed one another in grainy, black-and-white rather than begging or giving. "Okay, then let's narrow it down to American authors," Trudy urged.

Carlton jolted slightly and looked at Trudy. "You said writers."

Trudy was perplexed by the look on Carlton's face. "Writers, authors. What's the difference?" she asked.

"A great deal," Carlton responded as if defending the honor of one group over the other.

"Do tell," Trudy said, mimicking the formality she had picked up from a Bronte novel she had begun the week before.

"I am an author, having written and published just one work," Carlton explained. "A writer is one who cannot help themself. They must write as surely as a shark must swim in order to avoid drowning. Writers may or may not be published, but they cannot help themselves. They must write. It is, quite simply, who they are."

Trudy looked at her companion curiously, drinking in what he had said. "Allow me to rephrase," she said. "Male American writers. Whom do you admire?"

Carlton settled back into his chair and reached down and petted Roscoe absentmindedly. "That makes it a little easier, but not much," he said, the faraway look coming over him once more. "I like Steinbeck, Faulkner, Fitzgerald, Tennessee Williams, and Hemingway among others. Of course, they all pickled their brains, to say nothing of their livers," Carlton added.

"Maybe drinking is just something great writers do. Creative minds and all," Trudy suggested with a measure of hope.

This time Carlton remained staring at the stars. "If you're looking for an excuse for me, don't," he warned with an even tone.

"I just..." Trudy started.

"There are no excuses for what I did, Trudy," Carlton stated flatly. It was quiet for a moment until Carlton stubbed out his cigarette. He sat up as if something had just come over him. "Trudy, I think we should quit smoking," he proposed with an entirely different tone in his voice.

Coming out of the blue, the proposition struck Trudy as humorous, and she laughed. "Why? You only smoke one a day. That can't hurt you."

"Maybe not. But you don't." Carlton said, looking her in the eye. "Let's both quit."

It was clear to Trudy that Carlton was serious about the idea. "What about simple pleasures?" she asked slowly.

Carlton smiled for the first time since telling her of his downfall. "We can lean more heavily on the complex," he said.

"You mean literature," Trudy smiled, getting his meaning.

Carlton nodded. "The very same," he acknowledged. Trudy smiled and crushed out her cigarette.

At Carlton's suggestion, the pair started the next day by reading *Crime and Punishment*, a novel Trudy found initially difficult. She was unsure if it was her body craving nicotine as she gnashed away at wads of colorful gum, or Dostoevsky's language patterns that threw her, but Trudy often had to reread passages in order to glean any meaning. However, with discussions each night following agreed upon reading, Trudy soon embraced the challenge. With the help of Carlton's insight, Trudy began to read deeper than mere plot, recognizing themes, symbolism, and foreshadowing she had previously missed in the literature she had encountered.

42

The season that looked to be so promising nearly got off to an inauspicious start. Down by a touchdown at halftime, Coach Parson told Raymond on the way to the locker room that he would start the second half, replacing a teammate who experienced back spasms right before the intermission. Once inside the visiting locker room, Parson launched into a spirited speech designed to inspire and motivate. The speech was laced with timeworn clichés and stock platitudes about digging deep, fire in the eyes and belly, underdogs, and playing as if possessed. Raymond had never witnessed such a speech, but clung on every word as if it were gospel.

With the placement of the ball on the first defensive down, Parson faintly detected the same high-pitched, whirring noise he had heard the day he found Raymond logging the North Slope alone. The players looked around, unsure of the source of the whirring, the boisterous surrounding crowd noise confounding them. The sound ramped up considerably when the ball was snapped and didn't stop until Raymond had planted the quarterback in the turf. The suddenness with which Raymond had dispatched the massive All-Conference left tackle silenced the home crowd. Raymond's teammates broke the quiet with raucous praise, slapping him on the helmet and shoulders.

Once more, the high-pitched whine began faintly as the players lined up for the next snap. Again, like a small engine destined to burn itself out with excessive RPMs, the sound came on and crescendoed with Raymond stuffing the tailback who swept to his left. The next play resulted in a first down as the offense wisely ran to the opposite side. A review of the game film on the following Monday showed Raymond closing on the back, only to be clipped by the tight end.

A fullback was left to protect the quarterback, who dropped back to pass on first down. Raymond hit the husky kid so hard that he knocked over the hurler just after releasing the ball. The opposition called time out, and Raymond missed hearing the highest of praise from the bewildered fullback who left the field muttering something about a freak of nature.

Raymond made only two more tackles during the remainder of the game as he chased down backs from the weak side. Both plays resembled National Geographic programming depicting the hunting habits of a jaguar pursuing a small and hapless deer in slow motion. Raymond's defensive teammates picked up the slack, their job made easy and predictable by the offense's refusal to run to Raymond's side of the field. Following the game, each member of the opposition eyed Raymond warily as the players went through their respective lines slapping palms and muttering phrases indicative of good sportsmanship.

After the last player had disembarked from the team bus, Parson and Robinson sat in the front seat exchanging looks of puzzlement. "What the hell came over that kid?" Parson exclaimed, still wide-eyed. "I had hopes, but we never saw anything like that in practice."

"Good thing, too. We don't need the injuries," Robinson replied vacantly.

Parson could only shake his head and say, "Wow."

It was quiet for a moment before Robinson offered, "Maybe Raymond just can't hit our boys after they helped him the way they did."

The second half of the season opener put the rest of the conference on notice. Entire game plans were implemented and retooled in an attempt to avoid Raymond Gaines. Offensive lines were understandably jumpy around the deaf, defensive prodigy. The whining, motor-like sound unnerved them, causing the linemen to false start regularly. Running backs and receivers who had broken away looked over their shoulders for Raymond, who was known to run down both, his footsteps silent but the telltale whine announcing number forty-seven's closing speed. Players on both lines noticed the absence of steam or evidence of heavy breathing coming from Raymond's face mask, late in fourth quarters deep in the fall. As each game progressed, Raymond seemed to get stronger, double teams turning to triples in an effort to block the raucous defender.

Gaines' indefatigable speed and ferocity effectively cut the field in half, and offenses were limited. Opposing quarterbacks were forced to release the ball before their receivers were open, because they quickly learned that holding onto the ball meant having the whining noise stop six inches from their face as they looked up at the source who was only too happy to pick them off the turf in which he had planted them. Parson wisely moved his fledgling star from side to side making it necessary for offenses to exercise audibles. The chaos and confusion that Raymond caused could not be detected in a box score, but the conference buzzed of it all the same.

Some running backs are described as being 'downhill runners' because of the way they seem to carry extra momentum or gravity into a collision. The playing field being flat after a summer marching uphill with tons in tow, made Raymond a 'downhill rusher', and more than one opponent conjured illness or injury in order to avoid his wake.

Opposing coaches lined up their best offensive linemen against Raymond. None had the foot speed to position a meaningful block. Tight ends were paired with tackles to no avail. Raymond would split them like dry firewood. By the time Raymond reached a running back left to chip at him in pass protection he had enough momentum to pick up a spare, bowling both back and passer to the turf. Crowds swelled, scouts bustled, and headlines were made. The Coburn Cougars continued to roll over opponents week after week.

43

Trudy's school year got off to a strong start as well. So little known was she among the academic crowd and so complete was her aesthetic transformation, not to mention her overall demeanor and attitude, that most of her classmates simply assumed she was a new student. The '*A*' Trudy had earned in summer school had apparently vaulted her into the Advanced Placement English class for her senior year. It was in this environment, surrounded by her college bound peers that Trudy truly began to bloom. Holding back at first during class discussions, which centered on the course's first novel, *The Brothers Karamazov*, Trudy soon realized she had a lot to contribute. A point of no return came when Trudy expounded on the similarities between *Crime and Punishment* and *The Brothers Karamazov*, noting in particular, Dostoevsky's implementation involving the suffering of innocent youth at the hands of poverty-stricken alcoholic father figures. Trudy continued by shedding light on some of the common psychological consequences of murders that had been depicted in both Russian novels. This analysis was met with open-mouthed silence as Trudy's classmates instantly came to regard her as not only one of them, but someone they might look to for help with subsequent papers.

The level of confidence Trudy derived from her newfound academic status only served to further motivate her. After seeing how helpful reading Dostoevsky had been before being exposed to the writer's best known work, Trudy suggested to Carlton that they do the same regarding novels that were listed on the syllabus her literature teacher had passed out on the first day. Carlton could not help but to agree and soon found himself scrambling to keep up with the reading schedule Trudy insisted on keeping. The papers he critiqued for her continued to grow stronger in merit, logic, and conviction, as did the observations she began to make, increasingly unprompted by her current mentor, the former college professor.

No longer compelled to sit outside where they could smoke, Trudy and Carlton occupied a table inside the warm deli as they continued their literary discussions late into the fall after cleaning floors and tables on Friday and Saturday nights. As had become their tradition, the pair alternated reading pages aloud as they finished the last chapter of a book together. After concluding *The Sun Also Rises*, both closed their books with a smile.

Trudy shook her head. "Lady Brett could break hearts with the best," she concluded.

Carlton unwrapped a piece of wintergreen gum and stuck it in his mouth. "You'll do some damage of your own," he commented.

Trudy just laughed at the notion, failing to see any commonalities between herself and Lady Brett Ashley. "I don't think Bobby looked too heartbroken with Miss Bubbles on his lap," she remarked.

"Maybe not, but he seemed to be singing a different tune the last time he came in here," Carlton returned. He shifted in his seat. "Trudy, I enjoy our literary discussions more than you'll ever know, so I don't want you to take it the wrong way when I suggest that it might do you some good to be making friends and spending some time with people your own age. Maybe even go on a date or two, now that you no longer appear as if you like to drink blood," he teased.

Trudy had been tempted to say, *thanks for the permission, dad.* Instead she merely shrugged her shoulders and said, "I'll meet someone when the time is right. I know I will."

Carlton smiled sadly and simply said, "I'm sure you're right. All in good time."

When she looked at Carlton a somber look had replaced his good cheer and Trudy sensed he was thinking about his only child. "Is your daughter married?" she asked before she could stop herself.

Carlton looked at Trudy, chiding himself internally for being so transparent. He nodded.

"Does she have children of her own?" Trudy pursued.

Carlton looked embarrassed. "One, I believe," he said quietly.

44

To Raymond, it was the stuff of which dreams are made. He reveled most in the acceptance he found even before the attention and accolades began, reveling, in particular, on game days when he and his teammates wore their jerseys to school. From the first spring practice, he had felt part of something, been one of the guys. He had not been mocked, excluded, or made to feel different. The guys had pitched in to help him of their own accord. Around school Raymond smiled regularly as people signed phrases to him as they passed in the hall. That he didn't know sign language was perfectly fine with Raymond.

As was his custom, Coach Parson scanned the stands during warm-ups, prior to each game. If it bothered Raymond to be the only player without a parent in attendance, he didn't show it. Maybe it was a relief to not have to worry about another ugly or drunken incident. Still, Parson couldn't imagine not sharing the glory and success with his father as he himself had years before.

And Raymond's play made for plenty of glory and success. Perhaps no single play demonstrated the defensive end's potential more than the one in which he ran down a sweeping Terrance Wildcat running back from the backside, stripping the ball, and recovering it before running toward the far goal line some ninety yards away. Wildcat wide receiver, Billy Marshall, alertly saw the play and pursued Raymond, who had a five-yard head start. The crowd rose to its feet, most of them aware that Marshall was the state's hailing hundred-yard dash champion. The two sprinted down the sideline past the Coburn bench. Raymond could not outrun the speedy receiver, but he did not need to, for the sprint champion was unable to gain a single inch on the long-striding defender who had passed his cheering coach with a wide grin on his face and the pigskin under his arm.

As the final regular season game neared, Parson found himself inundated with numerous letters and phone calls from college programs. Some were regarding Tommy, but the lion's share were aimed at bringing the first year defensive phenom to their campus on a full scholarship. It was said that Raymond's potential was limitless given his enthusiastic coachable attitude and that he had so little experience playing organized football. College coaches and scouts didn't know what to make of Parson's contention that Raymond had never set foot in a weight room.

The redheaded senior had garnered a great deal of attention, with the spotlight growing brighter following each week's play, and Parson was impressed with how well the young man was handling the situation, which came with no small amount of pressure. Parson took it upon himself to make clear to Raymond that the opportunities involving his future were limitless. A college education was a ticket to live anywhere and do anything his talent and drive would allow.

Raymond quickly set aside the speculation that had begun to build by signing a letter stating his intent to attend Ohio State University. Parson only insisted that Raymond see the campus before signing, taking the highly sought-after recruit to Columbus on a Saturday following a game Raymond had dominated the night before. Walking around the university, Raymond confirmed his decision following lunch. Parson understood why when Raymond explained that his mother had likely walked the same paths and halls when she had attended the institution nearly two decades earlier.

College scouts were not the only ones to take notice of an emerging Raymond Gaines. Girls he did not know began to occupy previously empty desks near him in class. They became talkative and offered to help Raymond study as well as dropping hints regarding upcoming school dances. Raymond was congenial and warm in return but had long since developed a crush on Karen Stevens, who had relieved him of his red tangled locks in addition to silencing his squeaky ten-speed as summer had come to a close. Her growing affection toward Raymond mirrored the young athlete's rising star as the season progressed.

With Karen as his informal date, Raymond found himself invited to group events where established couples went en masse. Tommy was something of the unofficial ringleader and always ensured that a fun time was had by all, whether at the movies, devouring pizza, taking up a few lanes at a bowling alley, or hosting parties at his home when his parents were away attending Tommy's older brother's college football games.

At one such party Raymond found himself out on the back porch with Karen and a few other couples. It had felt crowded to Raymond, and he had suggested going outside, away from the noise and jostling of kids working their way toward a keg in the kitchen. Raymond had no interest in drinking and had been uncertain as to how he would handle the peer pressure at parties where alcohol was a driving component. Fortunately, while Tommy was happy to host these events, he didn't drink either, giving Raymond the courage to pass on the foamy plastic cups that people were constantly offering him at first. Sitting shoulder to shoulder, Karen and Raymond admired the stars and moon that were bright overhead. The other couples wandered into the house, and Karen looked at Raymond out of the corner of her eye. Raymond knew he wanted to kiss her but was not certain as to how to go about it and found himself wishing that he had asked Tommy for advice. When he glanced at Karen her eyes were closed, and she was facing him. Raymond closed his eyes and moved his face toward hers. Karen giggled when he kissed the bridge of her nose. "All this time and you end up kissing my nose?" she laughed.

Raymond was about to improve his accuracy when Tommy opened the back door and asked for help bringing a fresh keg in from his truck parked out in the driveway. While Raymond's strength was readily employed by the task at hand, Tommy took the opportunity to offer his inexperienced friend a point or two of constructive criticism, which Raymond was able to utilize when Tommy dropped Karen and Raymond off after the party. Tommy had elbowed Raymond, who was sitting in the front seat between Tommy and Karen. A slight jerk of the quarterback's head told Raymond that he needed to walk Karen to the door of her parents' home. Under the porch light Raymond remembered to keep his eyes open until his lips found their target.

45

The same night that Raymond's lips found Karen's, Carlton and Trudy lost their dog. Or rather, Roscoe had simply disappeared. After looking everywhere for the canine, Trudy sat in despair at a booth.

"Cheer up, Trudy," Carlton beseeched his downtrodden friend. "I'm sure he's safe, wherever he is."

"What makes you think something didn't happen to him?" Trudy asked. She began to spray glass cleaner on a smudged window.

"Oh, I don't know," Carlton said. He was wiping down the grill and had his back to Trudy.

"Well, what makes you so certain?" Trudy continued. She had not thought much of the dog at first and now realized how much Roscoe had grown on her.

Carlton straightened and gave a small sigh. "I don't know. I just got the feeling that we were but a stop along the way in a longer journey for old Roscoe."

Trudy stopped spraying the window where a child's greasy fingerprints could be seen. "What do you mean?"

"His paw was better, his coat was fixed, and he'd put a little flesh back on those old bones of his," Carlton explained. "I think we were something of a resting spot for the little fellow. A port in the storm, as it were."

"You think maybe he was on his way back to his real family, then?" Trudy's voice betrayed a measure of hope and innocence.

Carlton looked at his young friend and nodded as if he liked the idea of Roscoe having a family somewhere. "Could be. Could be." Trudy went back to cleaning the fingerprints from the window. "Of course, it could also be that he was sent our way as something of a reminder."

"A reminder of what?" Trudy said, her cloth pressed against the window.

"A reminder of the impact we can have on the lives of others," Carlton replied.

Trudy began to reflect on the impact Carlton had had on her over the past year when the man surprised her by adding, "Take you for example. You've reopened my eyes to the world of literature, Trudy."

"What do you mean?" she asked.

"Seeing these novels we've read through your eyes has been far more rewarding than when I first encountered them in my youth," Carlton explained.

Before that moment, it had never occurred to Trudy that she had in any way impacted Carlton.

46

The week of practice following Raymond's first kiss was one that saw the newly-anointed star on cloud nine, just as likely a result of his teammates voting him in as an additional defensive captain. His seemingly boundless energy had doubled, and it was accompanied by a nearly giddy enthusiasm that proved contagious. Coach Parson watched in awe as Raymond broke Parson's own school record with thirty-eight pull-ups, five better than Jack's best, set nearly a dozen years earlier. So buoyed was Raymond by his amorous heart, he actually intercepted a scrimmage pass Tommy threw to a running back coming out of the backfield. Raymond couldn't believe his good fortune and stared at the ball in his massive hands for a moment before running toward the far end zone. Tommy uttered the only curse anyone had ever heard from the quarterback, before taking off in pursuit of Raymond. Raymond looked over his shoulder and saw Tommy trying desperately to prevent Raymond from scoring a touchdown. The whole team laughed as Raymond ran backward the last twenty yards into the end zone. The exasperated quarterback tackled the cocky defender near the goal post, and soon the whole team piled on, laughing and cheering while both coaches smiled and shook their heads. At that moment, Parson felt his team was truly ready for anything.

Meanwhile, twenty miles to the north, conference rival, Roseburg High had been experiencing similar success with their vaunted offense leading the way. Scouted since his sophomore year was senior Ronnie Jones, a running back whose size and speed allowed him to run around, over, and by defenders. Experience had taught Jones that running over them early would allow him to run around them later. In a final game matchup whose winner would go deep into the state playoffs, it seemed destined that Gaines and Jones would exchange helmet paint.

47

Trudy was keeping one eye on a family who was using an abundance of napkins in their attempt to keep two toddlers' faces clean. The other eye she was keeping on a Steinbeck novel she was close to finishing when she heard a violent crash. It had been preceded by the squeal of rubber on asphalt as one of the cars involved attempted to brake a moment too late. The sound of steel colliding and glass shattering came next, and by the time Trudy had dropped her book and made her way to the door of the deli, Carlton, who was sweeping the sidewalk in front of the plate glass windows, was already pulling a child from the wreckage. The old man quickly removed his apron and used it to stem the screaming boy's bleeding.

"Call an ambulance!" Carlton shouted to Trudy.

The owner of an adjacent store rushed forth and exclaimed, "I already did. They're on the way!"

Carlton's face was flushed, and he was sweating profusely as he applied pressure to the child's wound. The apron he had been wearing was soaked with blood deep red. The boy soon lost consciousness despite Carlton's furious efforts.

"Come on," Carlton pleaded to the unconscious boy. "Don't die! Stay with me. Stay with me. Stay with me."

Trudy picked Carlton's glasses off the asphalt and kneeled next to the man as he maintained the pressure on the boy's wound. It seemed to Trudy like hours, but it could have been no more than minutes before a pair of ambulances arrived, their horns blaring and lights still visible despite the bright daylight.

When Carlton finally stood after being relieved by paramedics who tended to the boy and several others, the man looked as if he had aged ten years. Trudy got him a glass of water and sat with her still-shaking friend as he gave a statement to a pair of policemen who had arrived shortly after the ambulances. Uncle Fritz showed up soon thereafter and sent Carlton upstairs to his apartment to rest, assuring the nerve-racked man that he and Trudy would handle the remainder of the shift.

48

The big game with Roseburg was scheduled for a late fall Saturday night under the lights. The Coburn Cougars had Johnson's Café, which was owned by a former alumnus, all to themselves during the lunch hour. Coaches Parson and Robinson had a sizable chalkboard on wheels brought in and were reminding the different units within the squad of last minute responsibilities and strategies they hoped to see employed. The players were brimming with a confidence and enthusiasm that Parson wished he could bottle, with the ability to release it just before kickoff.

The idea of accompanying Tommy out to midfield for the pre-game coin toss, had elated Raymond to no end. It had been an honor and a thrill to just be considered one of the guys. Now, they had chosen him to lead, and it was a responsibility Raymond took very seriously as he looked around the café, drinking in the experience. Tommy Wilkins had the offensive linemen enraptured with a story Raymond could not entirely grasp from the next table. Pete Nelson, who had knocked Raymond over during his first spring drill, was replaying a tackle Raymond had made earlier in the season, the admiration readily apparent on the big kid's ruddy face. Coach Robinson sat at a table with another assistant coach, scanning the room, his eyes slowly floating from table to table similar to the way that Parson walked around the room shaking players' hands and reaching for a fry or onion ring here and there. Each coach was taking the pulse of the team in his own inimitable way, gauging the readiness of the group they had worked so hard to bring to the brink of a conference championship.

As he took in the entire scene around him sans sound, Raymond realized only one thing detracted from the potentially perfect day. The void created by not being able to share the day with either parent was not to be ignored. Raymond thought of his mother and how proud she would be of the progress he had made in terms of setting a goal and reaching it. He knew that Barbara Gaines would be proud that her son was going to college and insistent that he not squander the opportunity, that he come away with a degree that would position him for success well beyond the confines of Coburn. A tinge of guilt accompanied the void, and Raymond knew that his mother, if she were watching over him, would want Raymond to reach out to his father on this of all days. And while he didn't expect his father to respond accordingly, Raymond knew that reaching out would be a way of not only honoring his mother but dismissing the void inside his chest as well.

With three hours before the players were to show up at the high school for the bus ride to the stadium, Raymond went to Coach Parson and told the man he needed to go home for a while. Parson felt gratified when Raymond confided his reason and offered to give the teen a ride since he planned to stop by his own home for a bit of peace and quiet before heading to the high school.

It was mostly quiet on the drive up to the lone trailer on the hill where Raymond lived with his father. Parson felt a chill as he saw Daniel Gaines' battered, green Ford pickup parked askew in front of the dwelling. Raymond's father came to the door with a shotgun as he heard the crunch of tires on the gravel. A week's stubble adorned the man's face, and a dingy bathrobe over a moth-eaten sweater hung open as Gaines leaned against the frame of the door. Most shocking to Parson, even from a distance, was the black hollows around the man's eyes, as if sleep had been denied him since well before his last shave. Parson weakly put his hand in the air in a half-hearted gesture of good will. Gaines ignored the gesture and turned to go inside, the rickety screen door clanging unevenly behind him.

Parson was feeling guilty at the prospect of leaving Raymond for even an hour, but he sensed Raymond's determination to include his father in the day. Wondering if his star defensive player sensed his apprehension, Parson looked over at Raymond, whose hand was on the door handle. Raymond was looking at his coach, and it was clear to Jack that Raymond had something he needed to say.

"Coach," Raymond began with a voice that still sounded as if it came through a tunnel. "I want to thank you for everything you've done for me." Parson began to say something about Raymond making the team contenders, but Raymond put his hand up. "Neither of us knew that I could be a good football player, Coach," Raymond continued. "You got Tommy to get me to play.

I know that." Parson nodded, acknowledging the truth. For a moment the coach feared he would tear up when he saw that Raymond's eyes were moist. "You didn't tell my dad I forged the permission slip. I know that, too."

Parson nodded once again. He refrained from hugging the most feared player in the state and instead stuck his hand out to Raymond. "Coach Robinson will pick you up at five. Be ready, Raymond. You're a captain now," Parson said, looking Raymond in the eye.

Raymond blinked and shook his coach's hand hard enough to make the man wince. "Yes, sir."

Daniel Gaines brushed past Raymond's shoulder as he made his way out the door that his son had just stepped through. The man was wearing a worn Levi jacket and holding a pack of cigarettes in one hand and the keys to his dinged-up truck in the other.

"Where are you going?" Raymond asked in dismay as he watched his father walk toward the vehicle.

The older Gaines said nothing; instead he removed a bent cigarette and crumpled the now-empty pack, tossing it over his shoulder by way of response. Raymond stared from the threshold as the truck headed down the gravel drive and toward the nearest store that sold Pall Malls. Looking to change his shirt, Raymond walked toward his bedroom door but stopped when his eye caught a thick envelope on the laminated tabletop. The letter was addressed to Daniel Robinson Gaines, trustee for Raymond Robinson Gaines. The return address read George Z. Phillips, Attorney at Law.

There was a moment when a voice inside Raymond murmured not to touch the envelope. Raymond picked it up. It felt heavy. The voice inside him advised Raymond not to remove the letter. He pulled the thickly folded paper from the unsealed envelope. This time the voice screamed at Raymond, cautioning him against reading the contents of the letter. But Raymond could no more heed that voice's warning than leave an opposing quarterback upright.

In the span of a single paragraph laced with legalese, Raymond learned that the land he had cleared, rendering it virtually worthless, was to become his on Raymond's eighteenth birthday, which fell in a few short months. It had been entrusted to Daniel Gaines until Barbara Gaines' only child was no longer a minor.

49

Carlton drained the last quarter of his modest tumbler of beer and put the glass gently back on the table. It was clear from his face that the day had taken much out of the man. Trudy looked at her friend, more than a little worry for him etched in her own face as she extended a stick of bubble gum in his direction. While they were both well past craving nicotine, the gum had taken the place of cigarettes in their end of the day tradition.

"Thanks," Carlton said, taking the piece and unwrapping it before inserting it in his mouth.

"I couldn't find any Lifesavers," Trudy smiled.

Carlton almost missed the coy look on her face. "Cute," he said, smiling for the first time all day. "Lifesavers," he repeated.

"Well, you *are* a hero, after all," Trudy insisted. "You saved that kid's life. They said he's going to be okay."

Carlton studied Trudy's imploring face for a moment. "Let me guess. You think that today makes up for what I did in the past?"

"It's got to count for something," Trudy said, realizing she was trying to convince herself as well as Carlton.

Carlton folded the small wrapper and deposited it in his shirt pocket where his lighter used to be housed. "Do you really see life as a scorecard, Trudy?" Carlton asked.

"No. But I think the good we do gives meaning to our lives," Trudy replied with earnest.

Carlton leaned closer to Trudy. His eyes were bloodshot and his weathered face was blotchy. "You want to give meaning to my life?" he asked. "Go to college. Get out of this town. Break free, Trudy," he finished with a vehemence that further reddened the crimson splotches on his cheeks and forehead.

Trudy could sense something close to desperation in Carlton's words, and it contributed to her own. "Don't you think I would if I could? My family can't afford to replace our washer, much less send me to college," she said with feeling that easily matched Carlton's.

"Don't be so quick to give up, Trudy. There are all kinds of scholarships to be earned," Carlton said.

"A little tough to erase three years of academic mediocrity with an inspired senior year. Too little too late," Trudy said bitterly to Carlton, who had no response.

As if spent, they each leaned back in their chairs, the quiet next broken by the bursting of a large bubble Trudy had blown.

50

Nearly an hour later, when the captains, minus Raymond, were at midfield talking to the referees, Parson saw his assistant coach standing behind the far end zone. Robinson was alone and beckoned to the head coach. Parson knew it was bad by the graveness in his friend's face. Robinson swallowed hard, took his gnarled hands out of his pockets, and clasped them hard enough to turn the knuckles white.

"Where's Raymond? What happened?" Parson asked.

"Hospital. Boy's been shot," Robinson said tersely, his eyes meeting Parson's.

"No." Parson stammered, his face turning ashen. He did not ask how or even who else had been involved. "How bad?"

"Don't know. But the sheriff said it wasn't life threatening," Robinson said, looking down at the chalked line at his feet.

Parson balled his hand into fists. "That son of a -...," he seethed through his clenched jaw. "They arrest Daniel?"

Robinson shook his head. "He was nowhere to be found."

"I don't believe it," Parson said, shaking his head.

"Here's something else you might not believe," Robinson volunteered. "Sheriff said Raymond claimed he accidentally shot himself."

"Covering for the old man?" Parson asked immediately.

"Sheriff didn't sound too convinced. That's why he put out the APB on Daniel," Robinson said, looking down at his feet again. "We may never know what happened up there, Jack."

The players were not told of Raymond's injury until after the game, which they lost after giving up a season high two hundred yards on the ground and thirty-one points. Upon hearing the news, the team, to a man, insisted on visiting their wounded friend in the hospital, much as they had done when Raymond had been a prisoner to the North Slope just months earlier. The attending nurses on Raymond's floor had never seen anything quite like the scene involving nearly fifty burly teenage boys waiting patiently to see their fallen teammate.

Tommy and Parson remained after Coach Robinson and the other players left. "Does Karen know?" Raymond asked his teammate.

The quarterback wiped a remaining streak of black from under his eye and nodded. "She knows. I'm sure she'll visit tomorrow." Tommy glanced at Parson with a look that Raymond did not quite understand. Then he squeezed Raymond's good hand and quietly left the room.

Raymond looked up at his coach as quiet slowly refilled the small room. "I'm sorry, Coach. I'm real sorry about all this."

The machine that fed a drip line of morphine into Raymond's arm hummed slightly as Parson shook his head. He had forgotten about the game and realized Raymond was apologizing for the loss. "You've got nothing to apologize for, Raymond."

"I was a captain," Raymond croaked before reaching for a Dixie Cup that held chips of ice. When he was able he said, "I let the team down."

"You didn't let anyone down, Raymond," Parson assured the wounded teen.

"Still. We lost," Raymond said. "You said to be ready, and I wasn't."

Parson put a hand on Raymond's good arm. "Something tells me you came into our lives for reasons other than winning a conference title, Raymond."

51

That night, alone in her room and unable to sleep, Trudy acknowledged to herself that there was little chance of winning a scholarship even if she were admitted to a university. Still, some element of pride within her wanted to prove she was just as good as her peers who would be going on to college the following fall.

There was an additional reason she sought this particular goal. If there were a heaven, Trudy reasoned, Jimmy would surely be included. And if he were in heaven he would surely be watching over his little sister. And if Jimmy Thomas was watching, Trudy wanted him to be proud of her. If only for a year, Trudy Thomas would fly with eagles, she determined. She might never be able to boast of graduating from college, but Trudy vowed to at least earn an acceptance letter.

52

It seemed likely to Jack Parson that Daniel Gaines would wake up the following morning in police custody. If this was the case, it seemed wrong to allow Daniel's son to wake up in the hospital with no family to greet him after such a traumatic event, regardless of how it had really played out. So Parson had called his wife, Grace, asking her to bring him the novel he was currently reading as well as a sandwich and toothbrush. Grace had done so and left after providing her husband with a blanket and thermos of coffee as well.

Parson listened to the gentle pinging of a machine that monitored Raymond's heart rate. It reminded him of a stay he had once spent in a V.A. hospital, the nighttime quiet with the exception of machines and moans. As long and lonely as the nights had been, it was the mornings that Parson had always dreaded. For, mornings were when men would awaken and immediately reach for limbs that had been lost. The look on their faces told Jack that the men had hoped, for just a fraction of an instant in their waking moment each day, that they were mistaken in fearing the limbs had been taken, the fleeting notion little more than a cruel nightmare or hoax. Reality instantly set in and remained firmly in place until an uneasy sleep veiled the eyes of the wounded again after another cruel day had slowly passed.

Pushing the memories from his mind, Parson was able to escape into his book until he saw the hulking form of Sheriff Steve Davidson approaching through the window of Raymond's hospital room. Davidson peeked in the window and saw that Raymond was asleep. He hesitated for a moment before beckoning Parson to come out of the room.

The men exchanged a quick handshake. Parson had coached Davidson's son several years earlier, and the men knew and liked one another, with Davidson still a regular attendee at most home games. "Have you found Daniel Gaines?" Parson asked immediately.

Davidson nodded grimly. "Yeah. We found him."

"Did he shoot Raymond?" Parson got right to the point.

"Can't say, Jack." Davidson said. He looked down at the felt hat he was holding.

"You can't or won't?" Parson asked.

"Daniel Gaines is dead. Drove into the river out by mile post ten," Davidson replied.

Parson's eyes grew wide. "Was anyone else hurt?"

"So far as I can tell, there were no other vehicles involved, Jack. There were skid marks from Gaines' truck, but that's about it."

Parson's mind worked furiously to process the information, recalling Daniel with the shotgun on the porch as well as his own feelings of guilt in leaving Raymond alone with the haunted man. Sheriff Davidson brought his friend back to the present by asking, "How's Raymond?"

"He's going into surgery first thing in the morning, but he should be fine," Jack said vacantly.

"You staying with him?" Davidson asked.

"Yeah. At least until he comes out of surgery," Jack replied.

Davidson nodded. "You're a good man, Jack," he said, putting his hat on and turning to leave. "I'll be back after the boy gets out of surgery. No sense in telling him before he goes in. It'd probably make things easier if you were here when I told him," Davidson said hopefully.

"You're right, Steve. I'll be here," Parson nodded.

Davidson put his hand on Jack's shoulder. "Like I said, you're a good man, Jack Parson." The big man began walking down the hallway, leaving Jack to his thoughts.

"Raymond said it was an accident?" Parson asked, before the Sheriff had gone thirty feet.

Davidson turned slowly and tilted his head and raised an eyebrow. "That's what the boy said." It was clear from his tone and look that the Sheriff was skeptical regarding the claim.

Parson read both and nodded. Then he asked, "What about the river? That an accident, too?"

"Could be. But I wouldn't bet on it," Davidson responded.

"No? Why's that?" Parson was searching for answers, trying to make sense of a tragedy that continued to worsen.

"It was the same spot Barbara Gaines went off the road some ten years ago." Davidson tipped his hat out of respect for Raymond's mother.

53

When Trudy came home after her Saturday night shift at the deli she found her mother asleep on the couch. Dirk was nowhere to be seen, but Trudy guessed he was at a tavern or poker game with some of his buddies because Angela had fallen asleep while reading some of Jimmy's letters. Her mother never brought Jimmy's letters out when Dirk was around because he threatened to rip them up when she began to cry while reading missives from the son she would never again see. Trudy quietly placed a blanket over her mother and cleared a few empty brown beer bottles from the coffee table. She then began to refold her brother's letters and place them in the envelopes that were strewn on the table. When she looked at her mother Trudy noticed that the woman was smiling and wondered what it was that had given her reason to smile.

Under Angela's chin was the corner of a letter that Trudy had failed to notice while cleaning up. Trudy carefully tugged it free and sat down holding the warm letter to her own chest. The salutation did not include her, and Trudy wasn't certain if she should read it, not because her mother wouldn't want her to, but because Trudy knew the contents, whatever they were, would likely keep her awake.

Dear Mom,

This letter is for you. The much sunnier version is for Trudy Patootie. I didn't want to stress her out with this stuff, but I wanted to tell someone who wasn't a part of this living hell what we're going through. It felt as though a hand grabbed and squeezed Trudy's heart from within, just as she had known it would. She could hear Jimmy's voice as clear as pool water - he had used that nickname mercilessly. It had been meant to get under her skin, and it had, but nothing like the way it gripped her now.

> *I remember the looks when I first got here from the guys who had been here a while. They looked at us with contempt, especially the enthusiastic among us. These soldiers were ragged and unkempt with cigarettes constantly dangling out of their mouths and vacant looks on their faces. Some of them refused to talk to us unless they had to, and they never talked about home like we did. It's kind of funny, because I remember wondering what their problem was. Now, I look around at all the guys in my unit, and most of them look and act like those guys who greeted us with blank stares just ten months ago. God, that seems like so long ago. I'd say 'a lifetime ago' but that has far more meaning than you could believe since so many of those guys are no longer living. Of course, now I understand why they didn't talk to us. It's the same reason that I didn't want to talk right away to the guys that joined our unit after the bloodbath at _____ (They say we're not supposed to mention any places, in case our mail is intercepted by the enemy. If anyone is reading this letter other than my mother, I want to take this opportunity to tell such a person that THEIR MOTHER EATS KITTY LITTER!).* Trudy laughed at this, recalling

the line from a late night comedy show featuring Steve Martin that Jimmy had often stayed up to watch.

Anyway, the reason the old guys (imagine - me old) don't want to make friends with the new guys is that it hurts too much to make friends with some guy that will probably be dead or dismembered in a week or two. I learned that one the hard way, believe me. But the truth is, since our units merged we all get along pretty well and even have nicknames for each other. In case you're wondering, they call me Tom-Tom because of a sergeant that stutters, when he says my last name.

I'm back. Just pulled latrine duty. But I guess you didn't need to know that since you probably didn't even know I had left. Anyway, in reading this letter over I feel badly. I don't mean to sound so depressing. I guess I just needed to vent. I've only got two more months until this damned tour is over and I get to come home, at least for a while. I just wish I understood what we're fighting for. You see some of these poor devils (VC) after they're dead, and they're little more than skin and bones. They probably just want us to leave their damned country. Can't say I blame them, we've made a hell of a mess wherever we've gone. The bottom line is, I don't know what good I'm doing over here and often wonder if my time here will ever make any difference to anyone?

Okay, enough philosophy. We're getting set to move out soon, and I want to end this letter on a positive note – pun: get it? Letter/note? Parson Brown (we call him that 'cause he never swears) says I've got a fighting chance if I never lose my sense of humor. Most of the jokes the fellows tell are pretty dirty, but here's one he told me.

       The dad asks the son how his grades are. The son tells the dad his grades are underwater. The dad asks him what he means. The son tells him they are below 'C' level. I have to admit, I actually laughed. Tell that one to Trudy for me, Mom.
Gotta go, mail's leaving in five minutes.
Love,
Jimmy
p.s. Did I tell ya? I'm thinking of going to college if I ever get out of here. Some of the guys are talking about something called a G.I. Bill where the gov. pays for your schooling. I figure after what we've been through, it's the least Uncle Sam could do for us. Can you imagine? I'd be the first person in our whole family to ever go. Then maybe Trudy would go. Wouldn't that be swell? – you the mother of two college graduates! I don't know, might just be another rumor - but a guy can always dream. Right?

54

A few minutes after ten o'clock the following morning the Sheriff returned. Raymond was lying prone, trying to identify the book that was sprawled on his sleeping coach's lap when Davidson entered the room. The sound of the door closing woke Parson, who sat up causing the book to fall to the floor. Seeing Davidson, it quickly dawned on the coach where he was and what was about to transpire.

"How'd the surgery go?" Sheriff Davidson asked no one in particular.

Parson retrieved his book and stretched for a moment. "I gathered it went well," he said, before turning to Raymond. "How does it feel?"

"I can't feel a thing," Raymond replied. "I think I'm on some kind of pain killer."

Sheriff Davidson chuckled nervously. "You can be sure of that." He looked at Parson who stood up and moved to Raymond's side. "Raymond. I'm sorry to tell you this with all that's happened to you," Davidson paused, trying to find the right words even though he'd had all morning to gather them. He looked to his friend who stood on the other side of Raymond.

Jack nodded. "Raymond, Sheriff Davidson's trying to tell you they found your father," Parson said. Raymond looked at his coach, who continued. "He had an accident and didn't make it. I'm sorry, Raymond."

Raymond closed his eyes upon hearing this. After swallowing hard, he opened his eyes and nodded to indicate he understood. Nothing more was forthcoming from the teen, who simply clenched his jaw and stared ahead at his feet.

Nearly twenty-four hours later, Parson was also with Raymond when a surgeon told the young man he would never again play football because of the numerous steel pins now holding his clavicle together. The former star's despair was softened somewhat as Parson explained moments later that he and his wife were seeking custody of Raymond, a court hearing later that week to determine the outcome of Raymond's living arrangements upon his release from the hospital.

55

It was with the goal of a college admittance letter in mind that Trudy began to fill out applications for universities across the country regardless of cost, student population, or location. It was strangely liberating to write the essays that were often required, since she had so little to lose. The whole process served to further motivate Trudy as she continued to earn A's on her high school papers; grades that had translated into perfection on her first quarter report card. Because of the cumulative effect, Trudy posed no threat to those in the running for Valedictorian and other academic honors. It was probably a good thing for those students too, since it was Trudy they came to for help on any number of English papers.

56

The devastation of Raymond's dream to play college football came with an unexpected gift. Being welcomed into the fold of the Parson family served almost immediately to knit Raymond's damaged psyche in the same way that rest and eventually physical therapy would repair his shattered shoulder. The Parson children; Casey, Jill, and Timmy, took to their surrogate big brother almost immediately as Raymond absorbed the warmth of the family in much the way he had slaked his social thirst when the football team had befriended him at the end of the previous summer. It was this oasis of exposure to family bliss that Raymond later claimed allowed him to replicate a healthy and nurturing family environment of his own.

With the exception of Karen, who had visited Raymond in the hospital for all of ten minutes accompanied by a friend one day, the students at Coburn High welcomed Raymond back into the fold in a way that he had not imagined. Because of his size and growing notoriety on the football field, Raymond had grown accustomed to students and staff alike acknowledging him in the halls. The loss to Roseburg weighed on Raymond, who would always regard being voted a captain as his greatest honor. He expected his classmates would now either stare at him or shun him altogether. For some reason, likely tied to how badly he felt about not being there for the team, he had expected to become invisible, as if a blanket of shame and discomfort would enshroud him into something the students would rather forget. To Raymond's surprise, this was not the case at all, as both students and staff greeted him with smiles, nods, thumbs ups, and supportive pats on his good shoulder.

Raymond reasoned that the town's people likely landed in one of several camps regarding his season ending injury. There were plenty of those who chose to believe his father had shot him in a drunken rage. Just as many, Raymond knew, believed the story he had told Sheriff Davidson about accidently discharging the weapon while putting it away. Some people were certain the gun had accidentally gone off in a struggle between father and son. And then, there were those who believed Raymond had tried to commit suicide because of all the pressure resulting from the college recruiters. Despite the swirling of rumors, Raymond became relieved when it became apparent after a few days that no one intended to ask him about the incident.

None of which made it any easier as Raymond soon concluded that Karen Stevens was no longer interested in seeing him. She avoided Raymond in the hallways and was clearly uneasy around him when he tried to talk to her. For a long time he wondered if Karen's parents had forbidden her to see him. Maybe, as was suggested by more than one friend, Karen had no interest in dating a non-scholarship athlete. Regardless, Raymond would never be certain as to why the relationship soured, there being any number of rumors, just as was the case with his career ending injury.

57

"Your uncle said he's going to give you extra hours during your Christmas Vacation next month," Carlton said, as Trudy put on her apron. "He also suggested we liven the place up the week after Thanksgiving." Carlton pointed at a cardboard box with an artificial wreath protruding through an opening. "He dropped that off this morning."

"Ugh. Don't remind me," Trudy replied, curling her upper lip with disgust.

"What? I thought you'd relish the chance to make a little extra money," Carlton returned.

"Yeah. It's not that," Trudy said, as she wiped hardened pancake batter from a menu.

Carlton looked at her with puzzlement. "What then?"

"It's just that Christmas is so depressing," Trudy said with a disparaging frown.

"How so?" Carlton asked.

Trudy removed the misshapen wreath from the box and looked through a tangle of tattered garlands. "Well, last Christmas Dirk decorated our tree with empty beer cans. I spent my whole vacation waiting on my mother who slipped on some ice while she was drunk and broke her wrist."

"I see," Carlton said quietly.

"Of course, it was the same wrist that her previous boyfriend, Ricky, broke the Christmas before that when Ricky suspected she cheated on him," Trudy continued. "Which, of course, she did."

"Sorry I asked," Carlton said with sincerity.

"I think it was three years ago that our fine home caught on fire because someone, who shall remain nameless, fell asleep with a cigarette still lit in her mouth," Trudy said, her hands on her hips and her eyes looking to the ceiling with exaggerated recall.

Carlton saw the black humor Trudy was bringing to light. "I hope no one was hurt," he said, stifling a smile.

"No. But Mother of the Year, Angela Thomas, had to go with an entirely new hair style for about a month on account of some badly singed bangs." Trudy could no longer keep a straight face. Her laughter provided Carlton with the permission he needed to join her.

"Of course, the beautiful thing about Christmas at my house is that we don't have to waste any time putting up Christmas lights, since we never take them down from the year before," Trudy said through persistent giggles. "Nothing quite like Christmas lights on the Fourth of July," she added.

When their laughter had run its course, Trudy said soberly, "I could go on and on, but you can probably already see why Christmas isn't really my thing." Carlton nodded understandingly before taking the box of old Christmas decorations and placing it on a bottom shelf behind the counter.

58

The day after Thanksgiving Raymond found the Parson children to be quite enthused at the prospect of decorating for Christmas. "It's not even December," Raymond said to Casey as he watched the boy drown several blueberry pancakes in syrup.

Grace Parson brought a heaping spatula loaded full of pancakes for Raymond. "We like to get a head start," she said with a warm smile. Raymond poured himself some orange juice and frowned slightly.

"We're counting on you to help with the tree, Raymond," Jack said after washing a bite of pancake down with some coffee.

Raymond flexed his good arm for Casey, whose eyes got big as Raymond's bicep seemed to come to life. "I guess I've still got one good arm," he said.

"Dad," Casey said with admiration. "Raymond's muscle is way bigger than yours!"

Parson laughed easily. "All the more reason to bring him along."

Because of his long legs, Raymond sat in the front seat next to his coach. Grace sat in the back of the station wagon with her children, encouraging a chorus of Jingle Bells, Oh Christmas Tree, and Rudolph the Red-nosed Reindeer. Unable to hear, Raymond was lost in his own thoughts.

The tree beyond the Sheriff and his grim-faced father was small and scraggly as Daniel Gaines had refused to help his wife cut one that she would have preferred. After the Sheriff left,

Daniel had driven Raymond to the hospital where Daniel identified his wife's body. Raymond had been too young to understand the irony involving his father negotiating a road drunk that his mother had succumbed to sober. Raymond never got the chance to say goodbye to the woman that had given him life and seemed to understand him in a way that no one else had bothered. He had sat in the hospital lobby, staring at an artificial Christmas tree with blinking lights, while his father identified Barbara Gaines as his wife.

Back home, the scraggily tree was never again lit, and Daniel threw it, lights and all, off the front porch in a drunken fit of despair on Christmas night. On the way to the bus stop at the bottom of the hill Raymond walked past the tree - its needles brown, then eventually shed - for several months until Daniel pulled his son from school/Coburn in an effort to distance himself from demons, which nonetheless seemed to be waiting for them.

The station wagon and its off-tune Parson passengers eventually turned onto a gravel road and parked in a makeshift lot where other families were putting on galoshes and mittens near their vehicles. With Casey leading the way, Raymond and the rest of the Parsons made their way down a sloping hillside marked by perfect rows of shaped Douglas Firs ranging from four feet in height to well past ten. Naturally, the three children wanted one of the taller trees, and Jack and Raymond took turns with the saw they had brought from home while Grace took plenty of pictures. Trudging back up the hill with the tree, Raymond looked at his coach, wondering if the man was also remembering the last tree they had hauled up a hill together.

59

Carlton and Trudy were washing and drying dishes after a busy evening in early December. Trudy had turned on the neon light that indicated the deli was closed for business, so she was surprised when a man knocked on the glass door. She pointed to the sign in the window, but Carlton told her to let the man in.

"Do you know him?" Trudy asked hesitantly. The smiling man was rubbing his hands together and had large flakes of snow in his hair and on his shoulders.

Carlton straightened and twisted from side to side as if hoping to loosen his aching back. "Sure. That's Jorge. I told him to come by."

After Trudy opened the door, Jorge grasped the ten-foot tree that he had leaned against the brick wall outside. With Trudy holding the door and Carlton's help Jorge was able to jam the expansive tree through the opening with the already attached base coming first so as to not break any of the branches that sprawled horizontally as soon as the tree was placed upright. Carlton gave Jorge a ten-dollar tip, and the man wished them both a Merry Christmas as he departed.

"I thought we weren't doing Christmas," Trudy said, one eyebrow raised skeptically as she looked at the tree in front of the window.

'Maybe just a little bit," Carlton said sheepishly as he held his index finger less than an inch from his thumb by way of measurement.

Trudy frowned slightly, took off her apron, folded it, and put it in a drawer. "Suit yourself."

When she came out of the kitchen wearing her coat a moment later she was greeted by Bing Crosby's velvety voice dreaming of a white Christmas over the radio. Carlton was standing on a chair attempting to string lights on the tree. The piney, fresh smell of the large tree overwhelmed the various foods that had been cooked and served throughout the day. Afraid that Carlton would fall and hurt himself, Trudy relented, taking off her coat and pulling a chair to the opposite side of the voluminous tree from where Carlton stood with a line of lights in his mouth as well as his hands. They strung the lights from the top and worked their way down while Brenda Lee, Burl Ives, and even Elvis serenaded them with holiday cheer.

Trudy thought about putting her coat on again and leaving but gave up when she saw Carlton fumbling with tinsel, his arthritic fingers grasping and draping clumps rather than single strands of the finely cut foil. Surrendering to the spirit of the evening, Trudy told her literary friend to make them both some hot cocoa while she meticulously placed the tinsel so that it would truly look like icicles when the tree lights were turned on. After taking a break for hot chocolate, the pair resumed their work with Trudy following behind Carlton and making adjustments to the tinsel he still insisted on hanging.

It occurred to Trudy that the lowest point in Carlton's life had likely been the Christmas season, which had so drastically changed his life. He had merely listened earlier when she had expounded on past Christmases that she had experienced. Trudy reasoned that Christmases past had likely been no less depressing for Carlton than herself given the loss of his family and career following the fateful faculty Christmas party that shattered a number of lives. And yet, here he was putting his best foot forward in an effort to make this Christmas special.

"You do this kind of thing every Christmas?" Trudy asked while holding the back of Carlton's belt in an effort to keep the old man from falling off the chair and into the tree as he placed the star on top.

"No. Can't say as I do," he replied honestly.

"So what's the special occasion?" Trudy queried.

Carlton confirmed Trudy's suspicions when he stepped down from the chair and looked at her. "No one should ever grow up without knowing the magic of Christmas, Trudy. It may not be much, but with an imagination like yours, this tree may just serve as a portal to that same Christmas magic I once knew as a child."

"I don't know what to say," Trudy said, and in truth, she did not.

"I'll show you what I mean, if you've got time for one last cup of chocolate," Carlton said, pleading as much with his eyes as his voice.

Trudy smiled and nodded. "Two more cups, coming up," she chimed.

Carlton checked the various plugs on the tree while Trudy mixed two more cups. Simultaneously, Carlton turned off the deli ceiling lights and turned on the tree lights.

The pair sat at the counter basking in the simplistic beauty of the Christmas tree, each of them feeling a measure of warmth far greater than that supplied by the hot chocolate they sipped. Snow fell gently in the world beyond the tree and window behind it creating a life-sized vision that Trudy would forever recall when shaking a snow globe, or *portal to that Christmas magic she once knew.*

60

Raymond, his left arm still in a sling, and Jack brought the tree in from the garage where it had been left to dry overnight. More water was poured in the vessel that formed the base so as to keep the tree from drying out prematurely. The next hour was spent bringing in large cardboard boxes labeled "Christmas" from the garage. Raymond watched with awe, as nearly two-dozen holiday mugs were unwrapped from tissue paper, which was carefully set aside for reuse after the revered holiday had passed. Snow globes, wreathes, nativity scenes, garlands, holly, porcelain figurines, mistletoe, lawn figures, scented candles, Christmas books, dozens upon dozens of strings of lights, and countless ornaments - many school or homemade - emerged from the array of boxes as the entire family pitched in. During the course of the morning, Raymond saw the modest but always inviting Parson home transformed, as everywhere he looked the sacred day was commemorated in one way or another, all while Mrs. Parson managed to keep Christmas music and warm, colorfully sprinkled cookies streaming from the oven into the family room.

After lunch Raymond and Jack strung lights on the eves outside, with Casey taking care to see that no bulbs were broken as he guarded the lines that hung from the ladder to the walk or lawn as they awaited placement. Timmy and Jill supplied spare bulbs and plenty of advice to Raymond and their father. Electrical cords of all different colors and lengths were used to reach a mature cherry tree that Jack had always wanted to string with white lights.

Neighbors waved as they drove by, and Parson always smiled and waved back in a way that Raymond had never observed of his own father. The word *community* came to mind, and it dawned on Raymond how truly ostracized he and his father had become.

Community came to mind again as the family, minus Mrs. Parson, climbed once more into the station wagon and drove to a large chain store grocery outlet where they purchased more than a dozen frozen turkeys. They then drove to the back of a homeless shelter where Casey, Timmy, and Jill each lugged in a turkey while Raymond carried three more in a box supported by his good arm. With each succeeding trip, the smile widened on the face of the elderly man who had opened the back of the kitchen for them. When they had finished bringing in the frozen birds, the still-smiling man shook Jack's hand and thanked him profusely after handing each of the children a small candy cane.

"Raymond, this is Mr. Suminsky. He runs the shelter," Jack said, introducing the man who suddenly looked quite weathered and even older when his smile had run its course. "Mr. Suminsky, this is Raymond Gaines, the hardest working kid I've ever coached."

Mr. Suminsky took Raymond's good hand and said to Jack, "Coming from you that's quite a compliment, since most people have said the same thing about you since you were about yay high." Mr. Suminsky waved his hand a yard off the ground. Raymond smiled, his skin reddening at the compliment.

The three Parson children broke into a painful rendition of Frosty the Snowman in the back seat on the way home. "You've known Mr. Suminsky since you were a kid?" Raymond asked.

"His boy and I grew up together, played football," Jack briefly turned toward Raymond so the teen could read his lips.

"Are you still friends?" Raymond asked innocently.

The same look of weathered sadness came over Jack Parson's face that Raymond had seen on Mr. Suminsky's. "Phil didn't make it home. He wasn't as lucky as I was." Parson said when they came to a stop sign. His eyes locked on the asphalt ahead as the station wagon continued to move down the road.

A wave of shock cascaded over Raymond as he pondered the meaning to his coach's words. It had never occurred to Raymond that Jack Parson had served in Vietnam. There were no signs. The man was nothing like Raymond's own tormented father. How could this be? How could two good men go through the same meat grinder and one come out strong and whole, while the other emerged a bitter, broken shell of a man? What could possibly account for the different results? It simply was not fair. It made no sense, and for a fraction of a moment Raymond became angry and wanted to accuse his coach of lying. But the faraway look in the man's eyes as he stared at the road ahead made clear to Raymond that no lie had been told.

61

"Trudy, I propose that we push back our reading of *The Hunchback of Notre Dame* a few weeks, if you don't mind," Carlton said, after locking the front door a fortnight after the two had furnished the tree.

Trudy wrinkled her nose. "And may I ask why?" she asked attempting a formal British accent.

"You may indeed," Carlton said, matching her tone. He went into the kitchen and came back with a book that appeared to be quite old. "This, I believe, will resonate far better with the season," he said.

Frayed at the edges, the dark blue book was gilded with gold lettering that read "*Christmas Carol.*"

"Whoa, is that like a first edition or something?" Trudy asked. She set down the tray she was carrying and peered at the book Carlton had carefully laid on a paper towel he set on the counter.

"Pretty close," Carlton said, opening the book's cover. Inside was Charles Dickens' signature.

Trudy gasped. "Is that?"

"It is," Carlton confirmed. "My father gave me this."

"Wow. This must be worth a great deal," Trudy said in awe.

"To me it is," Carlton replied. "I figure if we read a stave a day, we'll finish up in plenty of time for Christmas."

Trudy smiled and began reading, "Marley was dead,..."

62

While putting away the last of the Christmas decorations after dinner one night, Raymond discovered a cardboard box in the garage with his name on it. He opened the box and discovered several dozen books, all classics. Inside the covers were his grandfather's initials and the dates, presumably when the man had acquired or perhaps finished reading each novel. All of the dates were decades before Raymond was born, enabling the nimble-minded teen to deduce that his grandfather had likely read the books when he was roughly the age Raymond was now.

When Raymond asked Jack about the books his former coach explained that the box was among the belongings he had retrieved from Daniel and Raymond's home after the judge awarded him custody of Raymond. The judge had remained dubious as to who was responsible for Raymond's injury and thinking it best that Raymond not be forced to return to the site, had granted Parson permission to enter the home and gather Raymond's belongings. Apologizing, Parson explained to Raymond that he had labeled the box with Raymond's name but had forgotten to tell him about it. Furthermore, Parson said some of the books were among his own personal favorites and suggested that Raymond read them while he continued to convalesce.

That night, alone in his room, Raymond went through the books and put them into piles on his dresser. He decided Jack was right, and that reading the books would somehow make him feel connected to his grandfather. Raymond had never been much of a reader and decided to start with something manageable as he located the three thinnest novels. Placing *The Old Man and the Sea*, *The Pearl*, and *Christmas Carol* on his bed, Raymond tried to decide which book to read first. The first two looked to be easy reading, but because of the season and Jack's compliment about his being a hard worker, Raymond opted for Dickens' famous ghost story.

63

Consistent with Thomas family tradition, Dirk pretty much put an end to the holiday festivities by shooting the television console while practicing quick draws with a pistol Angela had gotten him as a gift. Feeling anything but stupid, Dirk claimed the trigger on the pawnshop present was too light and needed adjusting. Angela started screaming about programming she had planned to watch and now stood to miss, apparently forgetting about the scheduling conflict of the previous year when Dirk demanded to watch bowl games on the same television that was now hemorrhaging a trail of acrid smoke. Upon regaining her hearing, Trudy suggested that quick-drawing indoors with a loaded gun probably wasn't a good idea and was shouted at by both Dirk and Angela for being less than helpful.

Suddenly Trudy felt the need to tell Carlton, who was the only one she knew who would appreciate the situation in the way that she did. Despite the deli being closed because of the holiday, Trudy found Carlton preparing the small restaurant for business the following day. Through the window, the man looked small and tired. He seemed to come to life, however, when he saw Trudy. A smile broke across his face as she turned on the lights to their tree and wished him a Merry Christmas.

"Trudy, I didn't expect to see you today," Carlton said, the joy evident in his voice. "What an unexpected surprise."

"I got the feeling there would be a little more Christmas magic here than at home," she said, taking off her coat and hanging it on the rack.

"Can I make you something to eat?" Carlton asked.

"Strawberry waffles sound pretty good about now," Trudy said.

Carlton chuckled as he fired up the stove. "Sure thing, Mrs. Renton," he replied under his breath.

"I heard that," Trudy grinned. She mixed a cup of cocoa, poured half into another cup for Carlton, and topped them both off with coffee from a pot that Carlton had already made for himself.

Carlton laughed heartily as Trudy reenacted the scene with Dirk outdrawing the television console. "I shouldn't laugh," he said. "Someone might have gotten hurt."

"Someone did, and I think his name was Curtis Mathes," Trudy giggled, referring to the prominent television maker. "I'm going to enjoy watching Dirk view his precious bowl games from a tiny black and white perched atop his latest casualty."

Carlton shook his head, and for a moment the deli grew quiet as he and Trudy watched tiny currents of air create a shimmering effect on the tinseled branches of the tree.

"I got you something," Trudy said, going to the rack where her coat was hanging. She placed a small book-shaped package on the counter between them.

"*Robinson Crusoe!*" Carlton exclaimed after tearing open the wrapping paper. "One of my favorites, Trudy, I assure you.

Thank you," he said, rising from his stool and heading toward the kitchen. "I shall put it in safe keeping."

Trudy heard him treading above her and knew that Carlton had gone up to his apartment. When he returned a moment later he came bearing a wrapped gift of his own. It was complete with a card, which came as a relief to Trudy, since it told her he had not just thrown something together as a means of reciprocating the gift she had given him moments earlier.

Trudy put her hands to her face as not even a gasp could escape her throat after seeing the antiquated Dickens' novel they had read together. Finally, she muttered, "You can't give me this, Carlton. It's too much."

"Oh, but I can, Trudy. And truth be told, it's not enough," Carlton said.

Trudy rose from her stool and embraced her old friend. "You should give this to your daughter," Trudy whispered. "That's who should have this."

Carlton held her close and returned the whisper. "Trudy, your heart's in the right place, but the truth is, my daughter's not really the literary sort."

Still embraced, Trudy whispered something she had promised herself she would not, "You need to go see her."

It surprised her when without hesitation, Carlton whispered back, "I know."

64

Raymond was awakened on Christmas morning as the three Parson children jumped on his bed and began to shake him. At first he thought the house was on fire. Then he remembered it was Christmas Day, and he looked at the digital clock in the dark.

"Hey, what are you turkeys doing?" he asked groggily. "It's only five-thirty."

"It's Christmas!" the children shrieked. "It's Christmas, Raymond!"

Still shaking the fog from his brain, Raymond shushed the noisy trio. "Quiet down, guys. You'll wake your mom and dad."

"They're already awake," Jill insisted. "They've been up for ages."

"Alright, alright. Give me a minute," Raymond said, stretching his long arms.

When he emerged in sweats minutes later, Jack handed him a cup of coffee. "Morning Raymond." Parson was unshaven and a bit disheveled himself, wearing a navy robe and clutching his own mug of coffee.

"You guys always celebrate Christmas so early?" Raymond asked.

"Hey, be grateful we kept them out of your room for the past half hour, Raymond," Grace gently admonished.

"You could have just started without me," Raymond suggested.

All five Parsons grew quiet and stared at the redheaded teen incredulously. "No we couldn't. You're part of the family, Raymond," Casey finally said, as if Raymond were daft.

"See?" Jill pointed at four bulging stockings hanging from the fireplace mantle, one of which had Raymond's name on it. "Even Santa Claus knows that, Raymond."

To say that Raymond was somewhat overwhelmed watching the plundering of the tree for the next half-hour would be something of an understatement. Mesmerized, he sat on the couch opposite Jack and Grace, who shared the love seat, watching the joy in the three small children's faces as they opened presents. Occasionally one would bring him a present, and Raymond would graciously open it to find a new pair of blue jeans, socks, sweater, or other such item. Before long he had an entirely new wardrobe to replace the dingy, worn-out, and all too often ill-fitting clothes he had been wearing.

The pine smell of the tree, the beauty of the lights, the taste of an assortment of candies, the warmth of the fireplace, the smiles on the faces of all; these things and more Raymond absorbed, vowing in his mind to replicate the environment for a family of his own someday. He looked at Coach Parson as more than a man who had everything: Parson was, in fact, a man who had emerged from a terrible experience and put it behind him as he made a great life for himself and his family.

After a breakfast consisting of sausage, Belgian crepes, popovers, and soft candied apples, the children bundled up and headed outdoors where it had snowed steadily throughout the night, leaving better than a foot of fresh snow. Raymond was given the choice between doing the breakfast dishes and supervising the children's play outside. Like any sensible teen, Raymond had hurriedly put on a jacket, scarf, and a pair of gloves he had unwrapped that same morning, just as Grace hoped he would. Soon Raymond found himself building a sizable snow fort, making angels in the snow, and launching soft missiles with and at the Parson children. Pulling the three children on a sled up a nearby hill using a rope, Raymond couldn't help but once again remembering similar and far less happy circumstances. How things had changed in six short months, he marveled.

65

As March approached, Carlton looked more haggard than ever, and Trudy began to worry about her friend. She had been tempted several times over the course of the winter months to once again broach the subject of a reunion with the man's estranged daughter. Despite the closeness they shared, Trudy knew that it was not her place to disturb this long-since scabbed-over wound and felt badly for having mentioned it on Christmas Day. It eventually became evident, however, that the notion had been plaguing Carlton as well.

"Trudy," Carlton began, as they washed and dried dishes together one evening. "I think I'm going to take a little trip."

"Oh?" Trudy asked innocuously.

"Aren't you going to ask me where I'm going?" Carlton prompted.

Trudy smiled. "I figured you'd tell me if you wanted me to know."

"Don't be coy, Trudy," Carlton returned.

"Okay. Where are you thinking of going, Carlton?" Trudy said, a slight singsong to her voice.

"San Francisco."

"Your daughter?" Trudy treaded lightly.

"I think it's time," Carlton nodded.

Trudy put an arm around her aged friend's shoulder. "I'm happy for you."

Carlton nodded and offered a slight smile. They were quiet again as they resumed the washing and drying of dishes. Finally, Carlton stopped, hanging his head as he leaned against the counter, his palms serving as braces as they spanned the stainless steel basin.

"What is it?" Trudy asked, fearful.

"I'm scared," Carlton admitted.

"Nothing ventured, nothing gained?" Trudy offered meekly.

"It's just that I don't think I could bear her rejection again at this point in my life," Carlton sighed.

Trudy thought about what she'd give to see her own father, just once. "She won't reject you. I just know she won't."

66

The collection of classics Raymond found was not the only discovery made from the boxes his coach retrieved from the teen's former dwelling. Young Casey was found playing with something he found in one of Raymond's boxes. Moments later, Coach Parson marched into Raymond's room holding the device in front of Raymond who looked up from *The Count of Monte Cristo*.

"Is this what I think it is, Raymond?" the coach mouthed to the redheaded teen.

"It's a hearing aid, coach," Raymond responded in his guttural tone. He looked confused when his coach broke out into an ear-to-ear grin.

"You mean to tell me, you can actually hear with this thing?" Parson asked, holding the aid in the palm of his hand.

"No. The battery's dead," Raymond replied simply.

"Are you kidding me?" Parson did not know whether to hug Raymond or chastise the mammoth teen. "A battery is the only thing that has been standing in the way of you hearing?" The coach looked at Raymond incredulously. "All this time?"

Raymond nodded, not sure what had his coach so animated. He did notice the next day, though, that a substitute taught the PE class he once again had with Tommy Wilkins.

67

Trudy watched over the top of her book as a family of four was finishing their dinners. A teenage boy was distracting his younger sister by pointing to various things in the deli and even outside the front windows. Every time the gullible little girl would look her brother would steal one of her French fries. Upon seeing nothing out of the ordinary, the girl would spin her head around, her blond, braided ponytail whipping like a cord each time. This played out at least six times, and Trudy found herself smiling until Carlton said quietly. "You miss him. Don't you?"

The boy gulped down another fry, and Trudy nodded absentmindedly.

Hours later, while they were splitting the evening's tips, Trudy asked Carlton, "You didn't mean Bobby, did you?"

Carlton looked confused for half a beat before a sad and knowing look came over his countenance. "No."

Trudy nodded, Carlton's admission confirming her suspicions. "How did you know my brother is dead?" she asked, skipping the question that might have come next.

"The evening you told me of your trip to the beach," Carlton explained, stacking quarters into two-dollar columns. "You used the past tense when describing your brother's sense of humor."

Once again Trudy nodded. "Okay." She sounded less than convinced.

"A lot of men come back from war without the sense of humor they left with." Carlton paused before continuing. "But your obvious affection for Jimmy combined with your failure to mention him again led me to conclude he was no longer alive." Carlton said these last words so quietly Trudy could barely make them out. Trudy stared at her hands until Carlton said, "I didn't mean to upset you. I shouldn't have said anything."

Trudy swallowed hard. "Actually, I'm glad you did," she managed. "It brought back a lot of good memories after watching that family."

"That's the spirit," Carlton smiled.

"I suppose that reliving fond memories is one way we can thank the departed for the influence they have over us," Trudy surmised.

"That and living to our potential," Carlton concluded.

68

The hands that had been unable to catch a football when Raymond had been a star player had improved from hours of tossing the ball with Casey, who had been in awe of Raymond since seeing the defensive phenom dominate games the previous fall. One early March afternoon following school, Casey and Raymond were playing catch on the street in front of the Parson home. Grace was preparing to take Jill and Timmy to piano lessons when she remembered something she had left in the house. Timmy, who wasn't thrilled to leave Raymond all to Casey, got out of the idling car and began to walk down the driveway to the street.

The car, which Grace had inadvertently left in neutral rather than park, began to silently roll back down the Parson's gently sloped driveway. When Raymond looked up after hearing Timmy issue a strange cry, he found the small boy pinned behind the passenger side rear wheel. The ball Casey had thrown bounced off Raymond's chest, startling the teen to action. Raymond ran to the car and put his good shoulder against the trunk of the vehicle, arresting its motion. Casey ran up to the car and got on his knees to pull his younger brother to safety.

"He's stuck, Raymond!" Casey yelled, his voice stricken with panic. "You've got to push the car forward so the wheel's not against Timmy's hip!"

Raymond could feel the weight of the station wagon pushing him back fractions of an inch, knowing it would continue to roll if Timmy were not wedged under the tire. The mind-altering effects of morphine had left Raymond unsure if he had dreamed or really experienced the words that he could hear Jack Parson saying in his head, *Something tells me you came into our lives for reasons other than winning a conference title, Raymond.*

Unable to see Timmy as he braced against the trunk and bumper, Raymond summoned his strength, controlled his breathing, and dug deep for whatever it would take to move the car forward. *Something good must come of this*, Raymond could remember thinking more than once as both the North Slope and his own body transformed over the hellish summer before. As the veins in his forehead and neck bulged, a sweat broke over his entire body, and Raymond's mind took him back to the previous summer when he had strained against many a log on an incline far greater than the one he now faced. The motivation he had often conjured in his mind in late August of the previous year had been that of hatred and anger: anger toward his father; anger toward whatever forces had conspired to kill his mother; anger toward a birth defect that rendered him different than other teenagers.

A grateful Jack Parson would later attribute the saving of his son's life to the adrenaline that coursed through Raymond Gaines, but Raymond knew full well that pure, unadulterated fury spawned the power that moved the two-ton vehicle forward long enough for Casey to drag his brother from certain death.

69

A tension Trudy had not anticipated hung between Carlton and herself as they waited for the bus that would take the old man west to San Francisco. It was clear to Trudy that her friend was filled with anxiety, and that he had slept little since making the decision to go.

Before boarding the Greyhound, Carlton turned to Trudy and pulled a book from his coat pocket. "I'm sure you'll grow to admire Francie Nolan as much as I do," Carlton said, handing her the novel.

She took the book in her hands as if it were a small bird. "*A Tree Grows in Brooklyn*," she said. "Thank you."

Carlton swallowed hard, and his eyes moistened. Trudy suddenly understood. "You're not coming back, are you?" she asked knowingly.

"I don't think so, dear," Carlton's voice cracked. When Trudy's eyes began to water, Carlton added, "I spoke with your uncle. He promised me he would hire someone closer to your age and a whole lot cuter."

Trudy laughed through tears that had no makeup to ruin. Carlton and Trudy embraced before Carlton tried to extricate himself from the hug. Before letting go, Trudy whispered heartfelt thanks in his ear. Not trusting himself to respond with words, the aged professor merely kissed the crown of Trudy's head.

Once again, Trudy had to laugh as she realized how small the pain Rochelle caused in leaving without a goodbye was compared to the pain Carlton's goodbye evoked. Tears flowing unabashed, Trudy waved until Carlton's bus could no longer be seen.

70

The evening of the day in which Coach Parson's PE class
had a substitute saw Jack's chair empty at dinner. Grace explained
to Raymond as well as her three children that their father had gone
to see an old friend out of town and could return any minute. After
helping with the dishes, Raymond played board games with Casey
and Jill while Timmy sat on Raymond's lap and watched. The
teen began to worry about his mentor when the man failed to show
up before his children were put to bed. Using a voice that had
become easier to understand since wearing his hearing aids again,
Raymond read the children several bedtime stories. They begged
their hero to continue reading them stories until Grace threatened
to turn out the light.

Raymond said goodnight to all four and retired to his room
to read until Jack got home. When he heard the front door open
Raymond bolted upright, spilling the nearly completed book that
lay across his chest while he slept. The grin on Jack Parson's face
as he shed his raincoat told Raymond something good had
transpired.

"Raymond, sit down. I have something to tell you," the
coach instructed his former player.

Raymond sat and smiled. "Good. I have something to tell
you, too."

"Give me a minute, Raymond. This is big," Parson said,
pulling the ottoman in front of the couch where Raymond was
sitting.

Raymond studied the face of his coach. "What is it, Coach?" Raymond asked.

"I drove to Columbus today to talk to an old friend of mine," Parson began. "Long story short, they're going to give you a job with the team. They're going to honor your scholarship, son."

While the scholarship that provided Raymond with the education to pursue a long and rewarding career was to change his life for the better in ways he could only then imagine, it was the last word of his coach's declaration that caught Raymond's notice, for he could never remember his father even once calling him *son*.

"You hear me, Raymond? You're still getting the scholarship," Parson exalted, clapping Raymond on both shoulders. Raymond just sat there grinning and nodding while Parson explained the duties Raymond would have in association with the Ohio State football program. "Now what did you want to tell me?" Parson asked after explaining Raymond's future responsibilities.

Raymond struggled momentarily to remember his own news. "You know your substitute, Mr. Barton? He's the track coach," Raymond began.

Parson nodded slowly. "Yeah. I know. He's a good man."

"Well, he had me run for him in PE class today," Raymond explained. Parson continued to nod. "He said I was a natural in the quarter mile. He wants me to come out for the track team,"

Raymond continued. "Said if his stopwatch wasn't lying, I could be looking at a track scholarship."

Parson leaned back, a look of wonderment playing on his face. "Wouldn't that be something, Raymond? Two scholarships in one day."

71

Trudy glanced around the austere office as her senior academic advisor, Mrs. Brandeberg, looked over a copy of the most recent report card in Trudy's file. The woman made small clucking noises as she read. Finally, the counselor looked over the glasses perched halfway up her nose and said, "So you think you want to go to college."

"I do." Trudy stiffened, readying herself for a pat response given to students who attempt to fool themselves, trying to fit in with those students who were clearly college material - who had, in fact, come from college material. The explanation given would make clear that the cloth Trudy aspired to fashion into a life among presentable people was simply not up to snuff. So conditioned had Trudy been all her life to expect such a reaction to people of her socioeconomic ilk that she was quite shocked when Mrs. Brandeberg took off her glasses and smiled at Trudy in a way that seemed entirely genuine.

"I must say. I've never seen such a turnaround in a student before," Mrs. Brandeberg beamed.

Trudy tried to respond but couldn't. She cleared her voice and tried again. "Do you think it's possible, Mrs. Brandeberg?" Trudy asked. "College, I mean."

"Oh Trudy, I know it is," the counselor gushed with conviction.

Trudy smiled and allowed to surface what she had promised herself she would keep buried. Hope that she might actually attend a university momentarily flooded her before ugly, jagged realities barbed the fleeting notion. Trudy bowed her head in acknowledgement of these realities.

Sensing a pall come over the young woman, Mrs. Brandeberg gently said, "Trudy?"

Fighting to keep the realities in check, Trudy looked up at the counselor. "A friend said you might know of ways to help pay for college. My family doesn't have much money." Trudy wondered briefly if Mrs. Brandeberg knew that *much*, in this case, meant *any*.

Mrs. Brandeberg clasped her hands together and placed her elbows on the file, which lay open on her desk. "You're not alone, Trudy," the woman said in a soothing tone. "Don't let money deter you. There are numerous scholarships, grants, and loans to be had, if you're willing to work for them."

"Oh, I am," said Trudy enthusiastically. Buoyed beyond any measure she had initially sought, Trudy thanked Mrs. Brandeberg effusively after the woman provided her with a number of resources and financial aid pamphlets. Trudy was opening the door to the woman's office when Mrs. Brandeberg asked, "Trudy, if you don't mind my asking, to what do you attribute your dramatic academic, and I dare say, cosmetic overhaul?"

Trudy blushed, and thought for a moment before responding. "A friend introduced me to the world of literature."

Mrs. Brandeberg smiled. "Might he be the same friend that visited me last summer and persuaded me to place you in the Honors English class?"

72

The morning following Parson's news regarding Raymond's scholarship status, the man looked out his front window to see the lengthy teen sitting on his front porch, shoulders slumped and head hung low. Minutes later, Parson came out with two steaming mugs. He sat down next to Raymond and handed him a mug. Raymond thanked his mentor before comparing the contents of the two mugs.

"What, no coffee?" Raymond said.

Parson smiled, taking a sip of coffee from his own mug. "It'll stunt your growth, Raymond," he said with a straight face.

Raymond looked at his coach, still not confident in the hearing aids he had begun wearing again after Mrs. Parson had installed fresh batteries. They both laughed at the thought of Raymond's growth being stunted. "You okay with what we talked about last night, Raymond?"

Raymond sighed. "Yeah, I guess."

Parson shook his head in bewilderment. "You guess?"

For a moment it was quiet while Raymond gathered his thoughts. "It's not that I'm not grateful, coach. I really am."

"But?"

"But. It's just that things are really good right now," Raymond said.

The realization that Raymond had recently lost both his father and dream of playing football made Parson wonder just how bad things had been for the teen to feel that things were now good.

"And things will only get better, Raymond. You will love the college environment. I promise."

"I like it here," Raymond said, looking into his mug as if expecting to see messages within tea leaves.

Parson nodded, his gratitude for the family he had freshly renewed. "Raymond, you know, we're still going to consider you a part of our family, even when you're in Columbus."

Raymond bobbed his head and turned away so that his coach would not see him fighting back tears. "Thanks," he finally managed.

Parson leaned back, propping himself with his arms slightly behind him. "College is going to open up a whole new world of opportunity for you, Raymond. You can study virtually anything you want, pursue just about any field. And I hope you do. But know this, your job with the football team is going to give you a lot of exposure. A lot of time to learn the game from some of the best coaches around."

"It's just a job." Raymond looked confused and almost annoyed. "I'll never be able to play."

"That's true," Parson acknowledged. "But then again, neither will I."

Raymond shrugged his shoulders in confusion. "I don't understand. What do you mean?"

"You picked up the game as quickly as anyone I've seen. And you did it without being able to hear," Parson said. "You've got a good mind for football, among other things," Parson added.

"There's nothing to say you couldn't come back and assist me with the team. Coach Robinson told me you could take his spot after you graduate."

An unbridled grin broke on Raymond's face as the coach continued. "Of course, before too long you'll be wanting to elbow me out of the way for the top job." Parson elbowed Raymond gently. "And by then, who knows, maybe I'll be ready to do a little fishing."

Raymond dismissed the thought that flashed through his mind as he was reminded of his father's temporary interest in the hobby. "Just a little fishing," Raymond responded, the grin still etched on his face. "I might need an assistant."

"Yeah, well, maybe ole Casey'll help you out," Parson said with a lazy drawl.

73

Confirmation of Mrs. Brandeberg's contention that Trudy was indeed college material came in the form of a letter from twenty-five hundred miles away. Philadelphia's Drexel University was proud, the letter said, to inform Trudy Thomas that she was to be admitted to their fine institution for the following fall. Standing at her mailbox in a light rain, Trudy looked to the sky and thought of Jimmy. For the first time, she felt certain he was looking down on her with pride.

Trudy retreated to her room where she pinned the letter on the wall after rereading it twice more. Then she got out her spiral and wrote Carlton of her news. After all, he was the only other person who had any sense of how hard Trudy had worked, and symbolic or not, the letter was the first of its kind received by anyone in her family.

When similar letters started arriving from states all over the country Trudy began to pin them up in her room, which saw the ugly, dark wood paneling slowly erode with each week's mail deliveries.

*   *   *   *   *   *

The times Raymond recorded in each week's track meets validated Coach Barton's assessment of Raymond's natural talent in the quarter mile. No longer toiling with anything that required brute strength, Raymond was slimming down, his build taking on the tone that befitted the quarter mile event, which required the combination of speed and power. With the Parson family and much of the Cougar student body cheering him on, Raymond also made it apparent that a track scholarship was not out of the question.

74

"He's not coming back, you know," Uncle Fritz said to his niece while they were closing down the deli.

Trudy kept her eyes trained on the stainless steel hood she was degreasing. "I know," she said after a moment.

Fritz sighed with relief. "In that case, I've got something I should probably give you." Trudy said nothing while her uncle went into his small office off the kitchen. When he returned he was straining a bit under the weight of a gallon-sized yellow mustard container. It was clear the plastic container held something other than mustard as Fritz set it on the counter behind Trudy.

"What's this?" Trudy asked.

"He wanted me to tell you to put this toward your car fund," Fritz said, cuffing the container and jostling the coins inside. Trudy unscrewed the wide-mouthed lid and peered inside at the multitude of folded dollar bills and hundreds of coins.

"What the-?" Trudy exclaimed.

"His half of the tips you guys split," Fritz offered before walking back into his office to retrieve his coat. "I'm guessing he saved it all."

"But I never even told him I was saving for a car," Trudy said, her voice trailing off as she realized her uncle was out of hearing.

When Fritz emerged from his office he was buttoning his coat. "I'm going to have to hire someone to help you, Trudy. I can't afford to spend this much time here," he said.

"Sure," Trudy replied. It was clear to her uncle that her mind was elsewhere.

"You can sit in on the interview, if you'd like," Fritz said.

"Hire whoever you want," Trudy said vacantly.

Fritz looked surprised. "You don't care who I hire?" he asked.

"It's not like you could ever really replace Carlton," Trudy said.

Despite the sadness in Trudy's voice, Fritz could not help himself. "I thought you said the guy was a dinosaur," he said, throwing Trudy's words back at her.

Trudy looked at her uncle and bit her tongue. She remembered the day she met Carlton and knew she deserved her uncle's ribbing. "That dinosaur was probably the best thing that ever happened to me," Trudy acknowledged.

Fritz began spraying down the sides of the stainless steel sink. "You aint the first person to say that."

Trudy stopped wiping the counters down and stood straight. "What do you mean by that?" she asked her uncle.

Over the din of the spray, Fritz said, "Guy was a war hero. Saved a dozen lives, from what I heard."

"He couldn't have been in the war," Trudy said tentatively. "He's too old."

"Not 'Nam, silly," Fritz chided her. "The second world war. The granddaddy of 'em all."

"World War Two? I don't believe it," Trudy thought aloud.

"Believe it. That guy stormed the beaches of Normandy. Fought his way close enough to a pill box full of Germans to throw a grenade inside. Otherwise those Krauts would've slaughtered half his platoon."

"I don't believe it," Trudy repeated. "Did he tell you this?"

"Are you kidding? Guys like him don't like to talk about stuff like that. But my source tells me that old guy's got a Congressional Medal of Honor to prove it. Not to mention a hell of a scar I'll bet," Fritz said with admiration.

"He was wounded?" Trudy asked, suddenly fearful for her friend.

"He was shot when they stormed the beach, almost drowned in the surf. Don't tell me you haven't noticed his limp," Fritz returned.

Trudy stood in shock, remembering Carlton's claim that he had almost drowned at the beach. This memory was followed by the words he used when she had asked if he had ever been to France. *Beauty plagued by misery.*

75

The Parson children brought out the liveliness in Raymond with their boundless energy and rambunctious play. After his shoulder healed, Raymond wrestled with the three endlessly, clearing out furniture for their theatrical bouts, where the evil, redheaded giant took on the three heroic bantamweights, as he called them. Grace marveled at how gentle the gigantic teen was despite their treating him like a piece of rugged playground equipment.

There were times, however, when Grace or Jack would come upon the young man, finding him quiet and removed. On one such occasion Jack offered to take Raymond to the cemetery where both his parents were buried. Raymond quickly said no, but approached Jack less than fifteen minutes later. "Is your offer still open?" he asked solemnly.

Despite the fully functional hearing aids in Raymond's ears, the drive to the cemetery was one without conversation. Raymond stared ahead, holding and occasionally smelling the two groups of fresh flowers the ever-thoughtful Grace had quickly cut for him when Jack had told his wife where they were going. Parson offered to wait in the car while Raymond took the flowers to his parents' graves. "No. You can come," Raymond quickly responded.

It was a statement of permission, but Raymond's eyes were pleading Jack to accompany him. "That'd be nice," Parson nodded. He did not understand Raymond's request but sensed it was somehow important that Jack go with him. The two men walked carefully up to where Raymond's parents' graves lay side by side. Daniel's modest tombstone had yet to weather the way Barbara's had, and it stuck out from the others. Raymond paused in front of his father's place of rest before standing in front of the slightly more impressive piece of granite marking Barbara Gaines' site. Raymond dropped to one knee, which soon grew wet from the moist soil, and placed both flower arrangements at the base of his mother's marker. It was only then that Parson understood Raymond's reason for wanting him there. Parson had remained dubious regarding Raymond's claim that his gunshot wound had been an accident but had never pressed the issue seeing that no good could come of it. Now Jack felt certain that Daniel Gaines had intentionally turned the steering wheel toward the river after believing he had killed his own son.

Raymond kissed his right palm and touched it to his mother's tombstone before rising to his feet. Shoulder to shoulder, Raymond and Jack stood solemnly in front of the graves. Finally, Raymond said, "I don't understand why." He left it like that, as if the sentence had run into a wall.

"Sometimes there's no rhyme or reason," Parson responded quietly.

"I don't understand why she had to die. Why it couldn't have been him on that road ten years ago." Raymond's voice was laced with bitterness.

"Like I said," Parson shook his head. "No rhyme or reason."

Raymond turned to the man he looked up to despite being a half foot taller. "Tell me this then, Coach. How can *you* come back from that stupid war without being affected, and *he* comes back a total asshole?" Raymond's voice rose in anger as he pointed at his father's gravestone.

Parson shook his head and looked Raymond in the eyes. "Don't think for even a moment that war didn't affect me, son. There isn't an hour in a day goes by that I don't fight back thoughts of my time in that hellhole."

Fighting back tears, Raymond gasped, "But you didn't come back a total monster! You didn't let it ruin your whole life! You didn't let it destroy your entire family!"

Parson swallowed hard to get past the lump in his throat. He put one hand on each of Raymond's shoulders and looked up at the tortured youth he had tried so hard to help. "Raymond, every man is different just like every tour is different. I don't know what your father saw or experienced over there. I don't know that I would have come back any different than he did if I'd been in his boots. Every second of every minute of every hour of every day over there was hell. Even when it was quiet and we were sitting around playing cards, waiting to kill or be killed, it was stressful. Some guys couldn't deal with it. I may have cracked if I'd been there one day longer than I was. Your father did *two* tours. I was injured before I'd even finished *one*."

Raymond's head began to bob as he nodded harder with each sentence Parson uttered. Jack knew the boy was looking for any reason at all not to hate the man he had so loved as a young boy. "I'm not making any excuses for your father, Raymond, but I saw men a heck of a lot stronger than I am crack under the pressure over there. I don't even want to think about what two tours would have done to me."

When the tears began to flow from Raymond's light blue eyes, Parson clapped him on the shoulders. "I'm going to let you say goodbye to your parents, Raymond. Take all the time you need," Parson said, before walking back toward the station wagon.

Raymond stood for a moment. He looked at his father's gravestone and tried very hard to summon a positive thought about the man. It was then that Raymond realized he would have stood no chance of saving Timmy Parson's life if Daniel Gaines had helped bring the logs up to the loading zone on the North Slope.

After closing the door and exhaling deeply in the shade of the vehicle, Parson saw Raymond coming down the slight rise where his parents were buried. Behind the young man, Parson could see that the flowers his wife had cut now adorned both Barbara and Daniel's gravesites.

76

The girl Trudy's uncle hired to replace Carlton was grateful to Trudy for taking her under her wing. It was symptomatic of the many ways Trudy had changed that she befriended the girl rather than ostracizing her for replacing a close friend in the way that Carlton had replaced Rochelle nearly a year earlier. Sarah and Trudy became fast friends, and Trudy began to anticipate a summer much like the one she and Rochelle had once planned. As much of Trudy's viewpoint was now seen through an increasingly literary lens, it occurred to her that things had come full circle.

It would not end there, either, as Uncle Fritz came into the deli with another gentleman wearing a business suit one early summer morning as Trudy was preparing to open shop. "Trudy, this is Mr. Silva. He'd like a moment of your time, if you don't mind."

Trudy looked at her uncle who was reluctant to meet her eye and knew something was amiss. "Certainly," Trudy said, straightening her apron and extending her hand toward Mr. Silva, who was holding a leather briefcase at his side. The man did not resemble the health inspectors that her uncle occasionally introduced her to, and Trudy grew concerned.

The man shook Trudy's hand gently and looked somewhat subdued as he smiled at her. "Maybe we could sit down for a minute?" he suggested.

"Of course," Fritz said, ushering them toward a booth where they all sat.

"Is everything okay?" Trudy asked, considerable alarm rising within her.

Mr. Silva nodded and adjusted his tie. "I wanted to start by saying that Carlton Smith told me he thought a great deal of you," he said.

"Carlton? How do you know Carlton?" Trudy asked, her pulse beginning to race.

"I was his attorney, my dear," Mr. Silva replied. "I'm sorry-"

"Was?" Trudy asked with alarm.

"Yes, sadly, Mr. Smith recently passed away," Mr. Silva responded with understanding. Trudy placed her hands to her mouth in an effort to stifle the gasp that came forth. "I'm sorry," Mr. Silva added quietly.

"Why?" was all Trudy could think to say.

"I can't say for sure. I am told he had been unwell for some time," the lawyer offered.

"But I just got a letter a week ago." Suddenly Trudy wanted to be alone. "Thank you for telling me, Mr. Silva. I don't mean to be rude, but I just need time to think," Trudy said beginning to rise.

Mr. Silva gently reached for her wrist. "I understand. But there's just one more thing I need to discuss with you." Trudy sat. "I believe you know that Mr. Smith had a daughter with whom he had been estranged."

"Yes," Trudy replied. "In San Francisco."

"And that Mr. Smith had moved to San Francisco in hopes of reconciling with his daughter," Mr. Silva continued.

"Yes," Trudy repeated.

"I am happy to tell you that his efforts were successful," Mr. Silva reported.

"Yes, he'd said as much in his letters," Trudy said, her eyes brimming. "He sounded very happy."

Mr. Silva nodded. "Yes. I'm sure he was."

"I don't mean to be rude, but I don't understand what this has to do with me," Trudy said.

"Right," Mr. Silva nodded. "In the settling of Mr. Smith's modest estate, I am responsible for conveying two items to you, Miss Thomas." Trudy put a napkin to her nose while Mr. Silva opened his briefcase and removed a document. "Many years ago, Mr. Smith began what he referred to as a college savings account for his daughter, Meredith. As you may already understand, Meredith and her mother moved some distance away after some troubles Mr. Smith encountered. Subsequently, for a number of reasons we have no cause here to explore, Mr. Smith lost contact with both Meredith and her mother, who, in time, remarried. Meredith's college was paid for by her step-father, who was quite well-to-do I am told."

Trudy merely nodded. "At any rate, the money Mr. Smith had set aside was somewhat forgotten and left to accumulate and grow, consistent with the investment vehicles in which it was originally placed. To make a long story short, it was important to both Meredith and her father that the money go to you for the purposes of funding your own college education."

Once again, Trudy gasped involuntarily when Mr. Silva put the tip of his pen on the figure accompanied by a dollar sign on the form he slid across the table. "And while Mr. Smith expressed a hope that you would attend a university far, far away, majoring in literature, he, of course, left those decisions up to you."

Trudy was rendered speechless, but her uncle was not. "You said there were two things," Uncle Fritz reminded Mr. Silva.

"Correct," the lawyer said. He wagged his finger as if to indicate he had not forgotten. "The second item," Mr. Silva said, pulling a manila envelope from his briefcase, "is this envelope here. I am unable to vouch for its contents, as it has been sealed."

Mr. Silva handed Trudy the envelope, which had her first and last name lightly scrawled across the face. It was clasped and taped shut, requiring that Trudy utilize a butter knife from the table in order to open the envelope. Inside was a manuscript written by William Stroud. It was entitled *Tale of Two Trudys.*

77

Raymond had walked the sprawling Ohio State University campus numerous times in an effort to familiarize himself with where his classes were being held. He did not fancy the idea of people gawking at his six and-a-half foot frame topped with bright orange hair as he walked into a classroom late. Having purchased the required novels at the campus bookstore beforehand, Raymond sat on the lone bench outside the building of his first class. The day was warm, but leaves had already begun to fall, and Raymond breathed in deeply through his nose, wondering briefly if his sense of smell had been at all diminished since he had begun using his hearing aids.

He had just finished reading the back cover of one of the novels when another student asked if she could share his bench. The girl seemed shy but determined. "I don't own it, I'm just looking to borrow it, same as you," he said with a warm smile. Raymond immediately felt foolish because the girl looked a little puzzled. After an awkward moment she smiled slightly, sat down, and pulled a book out of her shoulder bag. Both began to read in silence. After a few minutes Raymond felt her eyes upon his hands, or possibly the book they were holding. He looked at her book and realized they were the same.

"Are you taking Introduction to American Lit?" the young lady asked when she realized Raymond had noted her book.

"Yeah, Rizzo. Nine-thirty," Raymond said, pointing to the building they both faced. The young lady cocked her head slightly and Raymond could tell she was trying to account for the odd timbre of his voice.

"Me too," the woman said, extending her hand toward Raymond. He smiled, unable to remember a woman who had ever extended her hand in his direction. Her hand was warm and soft, but the shake was substantial, as if to say she was not only undaunted by his size but anything else this university so far from home had to offer.

"Raymond Gaines," he said with a smile.

"Nice to meet you, Raymond Gaines," she said. "I'm Trudy Thomas."

Epilogue

Dear Reader,

As you, no doubt, concluded many pages ago, Trudy and Raymond did indeed develop a great fondness for one another: a fondness that led to love and eventually marriage. You also might wonder what became of Coach Parson's offer to hand the reins of the Cougar football program over to his young protégé. As well, I imagine, you might speculate as to how Trudy eventually employed her talent for writing. Unfortunately, it's not for me to say in what remains of our time together. I can, however, assure you that Christmas in my parent's home was unfailingly a most splendid event, full of music, décor, wonder, joy, and most of all, love.

I can also tell you briefly of one of the more memorable Christmases we shared. It took place nearly a dozen years after my parents met on that park bench in Columbus. I was five or six years old, surrounded by my parents and Jack and Grace Parson, as well as their three nearly grown children on Christmas night, a tradition my parents enjoyed hosting as much as any other. My younger brother had brought out the brightly covered drum he'd opened under the tree that very morning. His play was evidently mesmerizing, or so I thought, because both my mother and Jack Parson suddenly grew quite silent. My father, using his customary deep voice, asked Jack Parson if he was all right.

*Jack swallowed hard and smiled. He pointed to the blue lettering on the side of my brother's drum, which read **tom-tom**. Realizing the rest of the room had become quiet, Jack, slightly*

238

embarrassed, tried to explain. "I once knew a man who went by that name."

Graces' eyebrows knit strangely. "Oh? You've never mentioned him."

A strange nostalgic look came over Jack Parson's face, and he looked as if he were far, far away as he blankly said, "I should have. He saved my life once."

My mother, who, as I said, had also grown quite silent upon gazing at the drum, turned to Jack with a start. "Where?" she demanded in a tone that was most uncharacteristic of her.

The attention once again shifted to Jack Parson. He faltered for a moment and then began to tell of a heroic encounter; one in which he and the lives of several other men were saved by a man from a unit that had been cobbled together with Jack's after heavy casualties had left both units depleted.

The End

info@michael-twist.com

www.ingramcontent.com/pod-product-compliance
Lightning Source LLC
Chambersburg PA
CBHW070606130626
46556CB00001B/288